Amos pushed it toward me. "You have certainly uncovered a very valuable treasure," he sputtered, his face red with exertion. "Ivy Towers, you have unearthed an actual Bonanza lunch box!"

"A what?" Sure enough, peering back from the top of the box were Hoss and Ben Cartright. I was pretty sure the green-shirted arm to their right was Little Joe. Well, unless the Lost Gambler was a lot more contemporary than the stories suggested, this hadn't belonged to him at all.

Other books by Nancy Mehl

In the Dead of Winter

Don't miss out on a single one of our great mysteries. Contact us at the following address for information on our newest releases and club information:

Heartsong Presents—MYSTERIES! Readers' Service
PO Box 721
Uhrichsville, OH 44683
Web site: www.heartsongmysteries.com

Or for faster action, call 1-740-922-7280.

Bye Bye Bertie

An Ivy Towers Mystery

Nancy Mehl

HEARTSONG
PRESENTS
MYSTERIES

DEDICATION

To Juanita Dunlap, who introduced me to the Third Person of the Trinity—and changed my life forever. God bless you.

ACKNOWLEDGMENTS

My thanks to Deputy Sheriff Robert P. (Pat) Taylor from Kingman County, Kansas. You brought Amos to life! Rick Brazill, Deputy Chief of Operations for Sedgwick County, Kansas. Thank you for responding to an odd e-mail from someone claiming to be an author. David Diamantes, a true "fire expert." Your help was invaluable. Ken Chau. I appreciate the help with Mandarin. I also want to thank you for the way you entertain my husband when you're both supposed to be working. But I won't tell. Susan Downs, the world's best editor and most patient human being. I'm blessed to know you. My agent, Janet Benrey. Thanks for hanging in there. Once again, I thank my family for their constant support and prayers. I love you!

ISBN 978-1-59789-766-2

Our mission is to publish and distribute inspirational products offering exceptional value and biblical encouragement to the masses.

Printed in the U.S.A.

I stepped outside the front door of Miss Bitty's Bygone Bookstore, a cup of steaming hot coffee in my hands. I could almost breathe in the approaching sunshine and joie de vivre of a fresh new season.

Spring comes slowly to Winter Break, Kansas. But when it finally arrives, the whole town blossoms. Doors closed tightly against frozen temperatures burst open much like the first fresh green blades of grass seeking warmth and sunshine. The townspeople put away their snow shovels in exchange for trowels and gardening forks. Flowering bulbs that spent the winter sleeping beneath the frozen earth are gently urged to life. Flora and fauna are welcomed with open arms, and life in the small town is colored with vibrant flowers and the sound of children's laughter.

"Hope you've got another cup of joe waiting for an old man who desperately needs his caffeine."

Dewey Tater, owner of Laban's Food-a-Rama, and the mayor of Winter Break, shuffled across the street toward me. He and my great-aunt Bitty had shared breakfast together every weekday morning for many years. Now that she was gone, Dewey and I continued the tradition. I looked forward to our time together. Dewey filled a spot in my life left vacant by my father and mother, who were serving as missionaries in China.

"There's plenty of coffee and some warm huckleberry muffins, fresh from the oven," I replied. I'd been working on a low-sugar/low-fat version of Dewey's much-loved muffins. Substituting applesauce and a little of Bubba Weber's honey for the sugar had proved tricky, but in the end, I'd finally found what I hoped was the right balance.

We followed exactly the same routine almost every morning. Dewey enjoyed hearing what was on the menu almost as much as I looked forward to telling him. For someone who'd never been a breakfast person, I was putting a lot of time and effort into creating special morning meals while making certain Dewey's food fit his new lifestyle. Diagnosed with diabetes, he had been forced to make a few changes in his food choices. In the scheme of things, however, this sacrifice seemed small compared to the loss of the woman he'd loved.

Dewey and my great-aunt Bitty had been what is commonly referred to as an *item*. If she hadn't been murdered inside her bookstore by someone she thought was her friend, Bitty and Dewey would have already been married.

"Huckleberry muffins, huh?" Dewey said with a grin. "You're getting mighty fancy for a girl who said she couldn't cook breakfast worth spit."

I held the door open, and the elderly man stepped inside. "Well, I can't allow you to start your day all cranky and out of sorts. Bitty wouldn't like it."

We headed to the sitting room located toward the back of the first floor, passing through the heart of the bookstore. Old books lined the walls from the floor to the ceiling. The smell of lemon oil, aged leather, and musty pages masked the aroma of my fresh-baked muffins until we reached the sitting room where I'd laid out breakfast on the big oak table used for town meetings and book club get-togethers. We could have eaten upstairs in my tiny apartment, but the kitchen was small and uncomfortable for two adults, although it was just right for one human being and a small calico cat. Miss Skiffins had come downstairs with me and was curled up on one of the overstuffed chairs scattered around the sitting room. Although the room contained a large fireplace that was used to warm the space throughout the winter, I'd left it alone the past few days. The mornings were still a bit chilly, but by midmorning the temperature was almost perfect. I'd started opening the windows so the mild springtime air and gentle breezes could sweep through the store, anointing it with the scent of wild honeysuckle. It grew in abundance in Winter Break, covering fences, lining sidewalks, and sometimes invading gardens where it wasn't wanted. But I loved it. To me, it was Winter Break's spring perfume.

My eyes gravitated to the decorative urn that graced the mantel above the fireplace. Designed to look like a book with a cross on the side, it contained my late aunt's ashes. Of course, I knew that Bitty wasn't really here.

She was waiting for us in a place even better than our beloved bookstore. A place where no one would ever be able to separate us again. But for now, having the urn comforted me a little. It was a reminder of the wonderful woman who had made such a difference in my life.

I poured Dewey's coffee from the carafe I'd carried downstairs; then I added a little cream and sweetener, just the way he liked it. "I still say seven o'clock is too early to be eating breakfast. Maybe you and Bitty liked to get up with the chickens, but I'd like to stay under the covers just a little longer."

Dewey chuckled. "Why, Ivy Samantha Towers, we both have businesses to run. You know that as well as I do. Breakfast at seven. Open at nine. That's just the way it is."

"Maybe for you, but why am I opening the bookstore at nine every day? Hardly anyone actually comes here. Almost all my business is done through the mail."

Dewey set his cup down and stared at it thoughtfully. "School will be out soon and you'll have kids wandering in. You know, Bitty couldn't stand to turn anyone away. Especially a child who wanted to read a book. Maybe the best reason you have for opening the store every morning is because Bitty did it that way. That's good enough for me."

I grinned at him and took a sip of coffee. "It's good enough for me, too, Dewey, but someday you're going to have to realize that I'm not Bitty. What happens when I actually do something a little differently than she did?"

He sniffed and raised one eyebrow. "You're already doing that. Bitty didn't take much stock in the Internet. Thanks to that nosy Noel Spivey, you're getting ready to put Bitty's business out there for the entire world to see."

I set my cup down and frowned at him. "Dewey Tater. First of all, Noel Spivey isn't nosy. His expertise with rare books has been an invaluable help to me. He's taken time from his own business in Denver to answer all of my dumb questions. To be honest, I don't know what I would do without him. And secondly, much as I hate to say it, this is *my* business now. Just because Bitty didn't know anything about the Internet doesn't mean I can't use it. I'll be able to sell more books and stay in touch with other dealers. It will be a big boost for the store."

Dewey took a bite of his muffin and chewed quietly, ignoring me. Finally, through muffin crumbs, he mumbled, "I'm just pointing out that Bitty didn't need the Internet to sell books."

I sighed and poured a little more coffee into his cup. "I don't intend to change the bookstore. I love it the way it is. I only want to make it as successful as possible so it can continue." I touched his hand. "Bitty trusted me enough to leave me this place. Can't you trust me, too?"

Before he had a chance to answer, I heard the bell over the front door jingle. I could have leaned back in my chair to see who'd come in, but it wasn't necessary. I knew who it was since he came by every morning about the same time.

"Any leftovers for a starving deputy sheriff?"

"Got a couple of homemade huckleberry muffins," I called out. "But if you don't hurry, I can't promise anything."

Amos Parker strolled into the sitting room, a big grin on his face. "Huckleberry muffins, huh? Sounds good."

Dewey smiled at Amos. "This gal of yours is getting quite proficient in the kitchen. A positive sign, I'd say."

Amos kissed me on the top of the head and pulled up a chair. "I knew if I waited around long enough, her domestic side would finally surface."

"Ha-ha. Very funny." I put a cup in front of him and poured some coffee into it. "Thanks to Bitty, I'm a very good cook, I'll have you know. But in my parents' house, breakfast was just something we stuffed into our mouths before we left for work and school. Dry cereal, hard-boiled eggs, toast, breakfast bars. . .that's about it. I've certainly been adding to my repertoire, what with Dewey's insistence on a 'decent breakfast.' "

Dewey snorted. "Those first few meals weren't decent. And they assuredly weren't breakfast. They weren't even fit for Miss Skiffins. Lumpy oatmeal and dry toast." He shook his head sorrowfully. "Bubba Johnson feeds his pigs better slop than that."

"Thank you for the encouragement," I replied sarcastically. "You really know how to inspire people."

Dewey grinned and shoved another piece of muffin into his mouth. "It's a tough job, but someone's got to do it."

I put a muffin on the small plate I'd set aside for Amos and handed it to him. "What's on today's schedule?"

"So far not much," he answered. "I have to drive to Hugoton and check in with the sheriff. Seems someone is picking up cows grazing near the highway and taking off with them. Also got some civil papers to serve for bad checks. Hopefully it won't take all day to find our phony-check writers." Amos took a bite of his muffin and followed it with a swig of coffee. "How 'bout you?"

"Actually, Noel is taking our Mark Twain letter to the museum in Hannibal today. It's pretty exciting."

"Hope you know what you're doing," Amos said. "You two could have gotten a lot of money out of that letter."

"I'm not sure I should have gotten anything at all," I said. "It was Noel and Olivia's letter. Not mine."

"But Bitty bought it from Noel's sister," Dewey said, reaching for a second muffin. "By rights, it was yours."

"Bitty bought a book. She had no idea the letter was inside. She would have returned it to Olivia, and that's what I decided to do."

"I'll give Noel and his sister credit for one thing," Dewey said. "Giving the letter to the museum took a lot of class."

"Yes. Yes, it did. When he offered to split whatever

he got at auction with me, and I told him I couldn't possibly take money made from Bitty's murder, he understood immediately."

"I think his grandmother's death sealed the deal," Amos said, taking a break from chewing. "What a wonderful tribute to her and to Bitty, donating the letter to the museum in their names."

"Bitty and I visited that museum when I was ten," I said. "It's a wonderful place. I'm so happy to be able to entrust Mr. Twain's letter to a place where it will be viewed and enjoyed by so many people."

"Why don't we plan to drive down there sometime this summer and see the display?" Amos said.

"That's a wonderful idea," I said. "I would love to see the letter showcased next to a plaque with Bitty's name on it."

"I'm sure you two young people wouldn't want to take an old geezer with you," Dewey grumbled. "Maybe you could bring me back some pictures so I could pretend I got to see it in person."

I chuckled. "Like Amos and I thought we could get out of town without you. Of course you can go." I caught Amos's eye and winked at him so Dewey couldn't see me. "Maybe we could invite Alma to go with us, too. She would probably enjoy spending a few days with a certain 'old geezer.' "

Dewey banged his coffee cup against the tabletop, his faced locked in a scowl. "I have no intention whatsoever of spending time with Alma Pettibone. I'm not interested in soap operas, and I certainly am not looking for a replacement for Bitty, even if she thinks I am."

I felt a little sorry for Winter Break's postmistress. She was a lonely woman whose family consisted of actors and actresses on her daily television serials. Although several people had tried to get her to spend more time with actual human beings and less time obsessing about the fantasy world she surrounded herself with every day, she continued to pass the time handing out mail in the Winter Break post office with one eye glued to the small TV she kept nearby. Recently, however, she had begun to show some interest in Dewey, much to his chagrin. Every time I picked up my mail, she would ask me how he was getting along.

"Oh, don't get so upset," I said teasingly. "You've got to realize that handsome, debonair men are going to attract single ladies."

Amos sighed and picked up his coffee cup. "She's right, Dewey. It's a curse men like us have to bear."

Dewey smiled, even though I suspected he was still a little upset. I decided it was an excellent time to change the subject.

"Isn't it about time to open that store of yours, Mr. Tater?" I asked teasingly. "I wouldn't want you to be a minute late unlocking your door."

"You just take care of yourself, Miss Towers," he said, smiling. He looked at his watch. "Got some beautiful watermelons in from Marvin Hostettler. You should come over and pick one out."

"Maybe I'll do that after I get Isaac lined up," I said, smiling. "Of course, I may have to push through the throngs of excited customers, but I'll try to find a few minutes this afternoon."

Dewey pushed his chair away from the table and stood up, shaking his head. "Since you think you're so funny, maybe you should try out for *Hee Haw* or something."

Amos snickered. "*Hee Haw*? How long has it been since you watched television, Dewey?"

Dewey grinned and shrugged his broad shoulders. "It's probably been ten years since I watched anything on TV except for basketball and football. It got so silly and full of garbage, I gave it up. I read instead. I've been through almost every book in this place—except those on the top shelves. They're next on my list."

"Good for you," I said. I didn't mention the small color TV sitting upstairs on my dresser. I'd brought it back with me from Wichita when I'd gone there to get the rest of my meager possessions. The truth was, I was anxious for Dewey and Amos to get busy with their daily activities so I could plug in the TV and adjust the rabbit ears I'd had to buy. Even though we could only get four channels in Winter Break, I was excited about it.

"I haven't gotten to those top shelves yet," I said to Dewey. "I'll start pulling some of the books down in the next few days so we can both go through them. I'll let you know when I get that far. Inventory is taking a long time because I have to research each one. I know the books on the shelves that face east are all valuable and for sale, and the books that face south are for reading, but I can't be sure that some of them didn't get mixed up since Bitty died. That means that each and every book has to be investigated."

"Surely Isaac is helping you with that," Amos said.

I shrugged. "Isaac knows a little, but he admits that his interest is more in what's between the covers of a book than in its monetary value. I think Bitty tried to teach him as much as she could, but eventually she gave up. Unfortunately, his lack of knowledge about what makes one book more valuable than another isn't helping me much right now."

"Well, I'm going to respect *our* differences and go open my store *on time*," Dewey said.

I waved my hand at him. "I didn't say I wouldn't open at nine. I'll unlock my door the same second you do."

"See that you do," Dewey said with a smile, "unless you want to be haunted by your aunt. I expect opening the doors at nine fifteen would cause an uproar in heaven itself."

"I'll remember. I wouldn't want to be responsible for anything that catastrophic."

Dewey chuckled as he ambled through the store and out the front door.

"I'd better get on my way, too," Amos said. "I'll check in later this afternoon. I have no idea what time I'll get back. How about dinner at Ruby's tonight?"

Ruby's Redbird Café. The only restaurant in town, run by a woman who had turned raising her customers' cholesterol numbers into an art form.

I shook my head. "I can't tonight. I've got to set up a special e-mail account and start letting Bitty's book dealers know how to reach me."

"Okay, then how about tomorrow night?"

"I don't know. What's the special on Tuesday nights?"

Amos grinned. "Tuesday's blue plate special is chicken-fried steak and mashed potatoes."

"Oh no. I have no intention of attacking one of those plate-sized fried wonders. Besides its being double-fried in who-knows-what, Ruby covers everything on the plate in mounds of gravy. Too many meals there, and you'll have to start rolling me around town. If I want to keep my girlish figure, I really shouldn't go anywhere near Ruby's ever again."

Amos crossed his arms and stared at me as if I'd lost my mind. Ruby's was revered by the people in Winter Break. I was surprised they'd elected Dewey as their mayor instead of Ruby. It probably had to do with the infamous Redbird Burger controversy. A pound of fried beef with extra sharp New York cheddar cheese, onions, and jalapeños mixed in and more cheddar cheese on the top, it sported a secret ingredient that Ruby wouldn't share with anyone. There had been many attempts to wrestle it from her, but so far, all plans had failed.

"Ruby added grilled chicken to her menu just for

you, Ivy," Amos said with a scowl. "She's bending over backward to make you happy."

"Are you kidding me? She grills chicken, all right. But after she cooks it on that greasy grill, she slaps melted cheese, green onions, and bacon on top. I hardly think that qualifies it as a healthy addition to her menu."

"Well, order a salad or some fruit, then. She's canned some wonderful peaches. You love peaches."

I sighed. "Yes, but the only way Ruby serves them is in a pie or on top of ice cream."

"Come on, Ivy. You're a wonderful cook, but I want to go out this week. I'm sure you can find something healthy at Ruby's."

"It would be easier to find the Lost Gambler's Gold than anything at Ruby's that still contains an ounce of nutrition."

"Well, people have been looking for that gold for many, many years. I guess that means you still have plenty of time to instruct Ruby on the finer points of wholesome eating."

I stood up and started stacking our dishes so I could carry them upstairs. "Do you remember the summer we dug up the peach grove looking for the Gambler's Gold?"

Amos chortled. "Yes, I do. The only thing I got out of it was blisters and a scolding from Harvey Bruenwalder. Filling up the holes was a lot of fun, too. Thanks for all the help."

I smiled innocently. "Harvey felt that young ladies

shouldn't be forced to do manual labor. I think that was very sweet of him."

"Sure. Especially since the whole thing was your idea."

"I have no clue what you're talking about. I distinctly remember that you were the one who was excited about finding George Slocum's treasure."

Amos shook his head. "You have a very selective memory. The whole thing started off with. . .'I just have a feeling, Amos.' "

I still believed the story about Slocum burying his gold right before an Indian raid. Amos and I spent an entire summer looking for it, but we'd never uncovered the secret treasure. The tale of the Lost Gambler's Gold was mentioned in several memoirs written by Winter Break citizens in the late 1800s. Rumors put it somewhere near the peach orchards outside of town, but it had never been found.

"Speaking of peaches," Amos said, "are we on for Ruby's tomorrow?"

"You have a one-track mind, don't you?" I said, sounding more irritated than I felt.

Amos pushed his chair away from the table. "I'll take that as a yes. I've got to get to Hugoton, but I'll stop by tonight when I get back." He kissed me and then strolled out the front door, looking a little too pleased with himself.

I didn't really mind going to Ruby's. I enjoyed the camaraderie in the restaurant. Besides church, Ruby's

Redbird Café was the place everyone liked to gather to check up on each other. I was getting a little tired of my own cooking, so going out would be a welcome treat. My problem with Ruby's centered on Dewey's struggle with diabetes. I felt responsible for him. I was committed to giving him, and the other citizens of Winter Break, a few options that didn't include melted cheese, gravy, bacon, slabs of butter, and fried coverings to everything—including vegetables. Ruby fried okra, mushrooms, cauliflower, broccoli, peppers, and even corn. She'd never met a fruit or vegetable she couldn't throw into her deep-fat fryer.

I took the dishes upstairs, loaded the dishwasher, started it, and then went back downstairs to get ready for Isaac. He worked Mondays, Tuesdays, and Wednesdays from nine in the morning until two in the afternoon. Unfortunately, there wasn't much for him to do yet. When Bitty was alive, one of his duties was to catalog newly purchased books. I wasn't ready to buy much, so for now, Isaac was helping me to inventory and research all the books on the shelves. I compared our list with Bitty's, making certain everything matched up. Although many of the books had an estimated value written next to their entries in her inventory lists, quite a few didn't. This meant I had to research their values on the Internet. Since the only service available in Winter Break was dial-up, it was a time-consuming and exasperating task.

I gazed up at the books on the top shelves, wondering

just what I would discover there. I was curious about them, but I was more committed to hooking up my TV. I had only a few minutes to get it done and then get back downstairs to unlock my front door. A few intrepid souls might actually wander in to borrow a book. Many times, visitors ended up in the sitting room, reading the afternoon away. Or, in some cases, catching a catnap with a book balanced precariously on their laps. But that was one of the reasons Great-Aunt Bitty opened her bookstore so many years ago. She loved literature and she wanted to share it with everyone in Winter Break.

I hurried upstairs and into my bedroom. It wasn't hard to get inside since my room didn't have a door. It was more like an alcove, really. The only real bedroom in the small apartment was Bitty's, and I had no intention of sleeping there. It was Bitty's room, and I wasn't ready to turn it into anything else. Anyway, I liked my room. It was where I'd always slept as a child whenever I visited Aunt Bitty during holidays and summers.

The TV was sitting on the dresser, and the rabbit ears were on the floor next to it. I pushed on the dresser so I could move it away from the wall and plug in the TV. When I did, I heard a crash. The gold jewelry box with the big, fake rubies had fallen off the dresser and landed on the floor. It was cheap and rather garish, but it was mine. Bitty had given it to me when I was little. Back then, I thought it was the most beautiful thing I'd ever seen. It had once graced my great-aunt's bedroom, but when she realized how much I loved it, she'd given it to me. Now, thanks to my negligence, it lay in pieces on the floor. I knelt down to pick it up. A folded piece of paper was sticking out from underneath the shattered jewelry tray that had been attached to the inside of the box. Although it was rather brittle and yellowed, I slowly unfolded it. A quick perusal revealed words, written in faded ink, that made a tickle of excitement run through my body.

It was a map. And in old cursive writing at the top were the words *My Treasure*. My conversation with Amos earlier that morning flashed through my mind. Was it possible? Could the story of the Lost Gambler's Gold be true?

Taking special care, I refolded the map and stuck it in my pocket. Then I cleaned up the pieces of the ruined jewelry box, tossed them in the trash, and finished hooking up the TV. When I was done, I ran downstairs and locked the map in the top drawer of my desk. I'd been enthralled by the story of the Lost Gambler ever since I was a little girl. In fact, the whole town of Winter Break was fascinated by it.

Could it be that the answer to the mystery had finally been uncovered? Was it possible that I would be the one to break the secret and find the treasure?

.

2

At nine o'clock on the dot, the back door of the store opened and Isaac Holsapple stepped inside. Since he lived in an apartment attached to the bookstore, it was easier for him to exit through his back door and come in through the sitting room.

Isaac was an odd little man, and I'd spent my childhood being distrustful of him. However, after Bitty died, I found out more about him. Many years ago, Isaac had caused an accident that killed Bitty's fiancé, Robert. Isaac's guilt had almost ruined his life. But Bitty had reached out to him with forgiveness and the offer of a job. Now Isaac worked for me, and we'd become good friends.

"Good morning, Miss Ivy!" Isaac sang out in his high-pitched voice. As usual, he was dressed to the nines, although his clothes reminded me more of something worn in the previous century. He always sported a long-sleeved white shirt with a wool vest. His ever-present pocket watch was in his vest pocket, the chain attached to one of his buttons. He looked like an English valet and acted a lot like the way I imagined one would act. Isaac was very prim and proper. Everything in his life seemed in perfect order except for his rather long, graying hair, which was always disheveled. I was curious as to why he paid so much attention to his clothing but didn't seem interested in taking care of his hair. However, it was one mystery I intended to leave unsolved. I wouldn't hurt his feelings for the world.

I returned his greeting, and soon we were knee-deep in books. Isaac would read the titles, check the inventory list for an entry, and then read the information to me so that I could set up computer records and research values and condition issues online. I tried as hard as I could to concentrate on our task and put my excitement about the map out of my mind, but it was almost impossible. I was certain Isaac noticed my distraction, but thankfully, he didn't mention it. Until I could find out more about it, I wanted to keep my discovery secret from everyone but Amos.

We plugged away all morning. By twelve o'clock, I was hungry and wondering what to make for lunch.

"Miss Ivy," Isaac said, interrupting my thoughts. "If you haven't already prepared something for our noon repast, I wonder if you would allow me to provide our meal." His smile told me he had something special in mind.

"That would be wonderful, Isaac," I said. "I'm afraid I don't have much on hand. I was thinking about going to Dewey's for some watermelon, but we could have that tomorrow if you'd rather."

He clapped his hands together and then scurried out the back door to his apartment. A few minutes later, he returned with a large covered bowl, two smaller bowls, and a couple of forks.

"I know how hard you're trying to bring some healthy foods into your diet," he said. "Although my own garden isn't quite ready to harvest, I have a friend who has a farm near Dodge City. His crops are weeks ahead of mine. I visited him Saturday and he sent me home with some wonderful things. I thought maybe you'd like to share a vegetable salad today."

I could feel my body leap for joy at the idea of fresh, farm-grown vegetables. "Oh, that sounds so good, Isaac. Thank you."

I went upstairs and fixed us each a glass of iced tea. I'd set a gallon-sized glass container of water with tea bags outside yesterday, letting it slowly brew in the warm afternoon sunshine. I preferred sun tea to the quickly prepared version made with boiling water. It took me awhile to get Isaac to try it, since he shunned all drinks with caffeine, but after I convinced him that I used only caffeine-free tea, he decided to give it a chance. Now he looked forward to a daily glass.

By the time I brought our drinks downstairs, Isaac had prepared our salads. Soon we were happily munching away on fresh lettuce, spinach, grape tomatoes, red onions, radishes, and crunchy cucumbers. Isaac's homemade balsamic dressing added just the right touch.

"Isaac," I said when I finally put my fork down, "what do you know about the Lost Gambler's Gold?"

He finished chewing and wiped his mouth with his napkin. "Honestly, Miss Ivy, I believe the story. I know it sounds fantastic, like something someone made up, but after studying various accounts, I'm convinced it's true."

"I'd love to hear what you've learned. Except for reading a few old memoirs, my only knowledge comes from the tall tales we kids used to tell each other during slumber parties or late-night excursions into the peach orchard. We weren't really going for historical accuracy."

Isaac leaned forward a little, seemingly prodded by my encouragement. "According to stories written by the early settlers of Winter Break, George Slocum was a gambler on his way back east where he was born and raised. Supposedly he'd won a fortune in gold from a miner who'd struck it rich during the great gold rush of the 1860s."

"Was that in Colorado?" I asked.

"Well, the first gold rush occurred in California, but in 1859, gold was found in what is now known as Colorado. Of course, then it was actually a part of the Kansas Territory. Colorado Territory was established in 1861."

I shook my head. "My goodness, Isaac. You're a walking history book."

He smiled. "Now, Miss Ivy, I've been working in this bookstore for over forty years. What do you think I do in my spare time? I've read almost everything that's ever passed through this wonderful place. Books can teach you so many things." He sighed. "I truly feel sorry for people who don't read."

"Back to George Slocum. . . ," I gently reminded him.

"Oh yes, now where was I?"

"He was on his way back east."

"Yes. It was 1861. Fort Sumter had been attacked by Confederate troops and the Civil War had begun. Slocum wanted to get back to Kentucky before the fighting escalated. He stopped in Winter Break to rest his horse for a couple of days before continuing home. Unfortunately, news of an imminent attack from a tribe of Indians forced him to change his plans. Fearing that his gold would be stolen, he buried it and then joined with Winter Break residents to stand against the Indians. Although the town was saved, Slocum was lost." Isaac took a sip of iced tea and smiled at me. Then he lowered his voice to a conspiratorial whisper. "The rumor was that he wasn't actually killed by an Indian arrow, but instead by a Winter Break citizen who knew about the gold." He shrugged and waved a hand in the air. "But who knows?" he said with a final flourish. "Whether the person who killed George Slocum found the gold is impossible to know. Town gossip says it was never discovered. Thus began the legend of the Lost Gambler's Gold."

"And the stories we kids used to tell each other."

Isaac chuckled. "Oh, you mean about the Gambler's ghostly hand reaching up from under the ground to drag you down to his grave?"

"Yes. I had a few nightmares because of it, let me tell you." I shuddered at the memory.

Isaac stacked our empty salad bowls and stood up. "I'll take these back to my apartment; then we'll get started again." He headed toward the back door but stopped before reaching it. "I hope I answered your question."

I grinned at him. "Goodness, Isaac. I learned more from you in a few minutes than I have from years of listening to childish rumors and reading old memoirs."

He nodded with satisfaction. "Good. Of course, you know there isn't likely to be any treasure still buried here, don't you?"

"Why do you say that?"

He looked at me with amusement. "Why, Miss Ivy, I doubt that Mr. Slocum had much time to bury his treasure. That would mean it wasn't too far from the surface. This is primarily a farming community. After all this time, someone plowing a field would surely have found it. Most probably, however, someone saw Slocum with his gold and killed him for it. It's probably long gone by now."

As the door closed behind him, I began to ponder the logic of his conclusion. I truly hoped he was wrong. I could hardly wait to show the map to Amos and get his opinion. Even more exciting was the idea of following the map and digging at the spot marked with a big red X.

Isaac and I worked diligently the rest of the afternoon. At two o'clock, he went home, leaving me some time to look a little more closely at the mysterious map. Before I had a chance to take it out of my desk, the bell over the front door tinkled, and Alma Pettibone stepped in. She glanced nervously around the store until her gaze rested on me. I was surprised to see her for two reasons. First of all because she never left the post office during the day due to what she called her "important postal duties" and second because her soaps weren't over until three o'clock.

"Ivy!" she said rather breathlessly. She reached up with one hand and tried to tug her silver hair back into its original topknot. It must have come undone in her hurry to get across the street. "I just had to bring this to you right away. The postmark says *China*!"

I got up from the desk and took the letter from her. Sure enough, it had come all the way from Hong Kong. But why would my parents write to me instead of calling? The handwriting on the envelope was definitely my mother's. "Thanks, Alma," I said. "It's from my mother and father. I think I told you they're missionaries overseas."

"Yes, dear. I do remember. But why would they mail you a letter? I mean, even at Christmas they didn't send anything."

"My parents won't send packages from China," I said. "It's very expensive, and many times, items are lost along the way."

Alma looked at me sympathetically. "I'm sure that's it, dear," she said.

I thought about defending myself by assuring her that my parents didn't ignore me at Christmas because they didn't love me but realized I was getting sidetracked. I wanted to read my letter. In private.

"Thanks for bringing it over, Alma," I said, scooting behind her so I could hold the door open. "I really appreciate it."

She paused for a moment and stared at the envelope in my hand. I knew she wanted me to read it in her presence, but I had no intention of doing so. Finally, she threw me a forced smile and hurried back to her precious afternoon serials. I waited until I saw her enter the post office; then I took the letter back to my desk and opened it. It wasn't until I reached the third paragraph that I discovered the real reason my mother had sent me a letter instead of calling.

We are taking a brief sabbatical so we can spend some time with you in Winter Break. Recent decisions you've made have caused us quite a bit of concern, Ivy. We want to make absolutely certain you haven't embarked upon a path that will bring you great heartache.

We will arrive in Wichita on the sixteenth and then rent a car and drive to Winter Break. We will arrive in town on the seventeenth. Don't worry about accommodations; we've already made arrangements.

I hope you will be glad to see us. We certainly are looking forward to being with you.

Love,
Mother

The seventeenth? Things move a little slowly in Winter Break, and for the life of me, I couldn't remember today's date. I flipped open my day planner and scanned the calendar. Today was the fifteenth! They would be here in two days. My mother hadn't warned me earlier about their visit because she knew I would have tried to talk her out of it. Now it was too late. They'd already left China.

Miss Skiffins ambled up next to me and rubbed my leg. I picked her up and buried my face in her soft fur. "We'd better get all our ducks in a row, sweetie. In a couple of days we're going to war." I didn't mean literal combat, but there would certainly be an emotional battle for my future. My mother had not accepted my decision to move to Winter Break with grace. She saw my choice to stay here and continue Aunt Bitty's bookstore as an act of rebellion. My mother wanted me to join her and my father in China. Although I respected their commitment to evangelism, I didn't feel it was the place God called me to be. My efforts to convince them of that obviously hadn't been successful.

I wondered where they planned to stay. Since there weren't any motels in Winter Break, the closest they could get would be Hugoton. It wasn't much, but at least there would be a little distance between us. A gentle swat with her fluffy paw told me Miss Skiffins had been squeezed enough for a while. I put her down and turned my attention to the treasure map. There was nothing I could do at that moment about my parents, so I tried to push worry from my mind by focusing on the possibility of finding long-hidden gold.

I took the map from its hiding place and carefully smoothed it out. Winter Break was drawn as a series of small squares. The road out of town wound past the graveyard and toward the peach orchards. In the middle of the orchards, there was an object sketched in. It was round with tiny lines inside its borders. There were words written next to it, but they were so smudged I couldn't make them out. From that point, tiny footprints had been drawn, each one heading north, until they stopped at an object marked with a large red X.

"X marks the spot," I said softly to myself. As I felt a rush of excitement about the map, seeds of worry also crept into my mind. The Lost Gambler's Gold had held on to its resting place for a long time. Would I be as tenacious when my mother tried to uproot me from Winter Break? I steeled myself for what lay ahead, asking God for the courage to stand strong and to hold on to the life I believed He'd called me to live.

3

By early evening, dark clouds began to gather over Winter Break. I'd spent the afternoon going over the account books on the big table in the sitting room. I closed the last one and checked my watch. I had plans to pop some popcorn and watch a little TV before bed. It sounded like a perfect plan for a rainy night. Although I had a few favorite shows, I tried to watch television sparingly. Bitty had never owned a "mind trap," as she called all television sets, and I'd never really noticed its absence during our summers and holidays together. She'd told me more than once that a good book was much more beneficial to the brain than TV. "Books activate thought and imagination, Ivy," she'd say. "TV on—imagination off." Although I hadn't adapted my life to her choice of no TV at all, I certainly wasn't planning to emulate Alma Pettibone by getting stuck on certain programs and allowing them to run my life. I intended to exercise one of the most difficult but necessary fruits of the Spirit: self-control.

I was stacking the account books in a neat pile when I heard the front door open. Stretching, I got up to see who it was and found Amos standing on the landing. I expected to see his usual smile. Instead I discovered a decidedly somber expression.

"What's wrong?" I asked.

When he didn't answer, I hurried over to my desk and sat down, motioning to the chair next to me. I could hardly wait to show him the map. He sat down with a grunt, his forehead creased with worry. "You remember those cows I told you about?" he said finally. "The ones being stolen?"

I nodded.

"It's become an epidemic. Cows are disappearing all over the place."

"Maybe it's aliens," I said, trying not to smile. "I saw something on TV once—"

"It's not funny, Ivy," Amos said in a low voice. "I think we may know one of the people involved."

I pulled the map out of my drawer and put it on top of the desk, waiting for the cow conversation to end so I could show it to him. "Who do you think it is?"

Amos sighed. "The description I got matches Odie Rimrucker."

I couldn't keep the indignation out of my voice. "Amos! It couldn't be Odie. He'd never do anything like that."

He nodded, but his expression didn't change. "I know what you're saying, but it sounds just like him. Even down to a description of his truck."

I couldn't believe it. At one time, Odie had been the town drunk. He'd lost his family, his job, and most of his friends to drinking. But several years ago my aunt Bitty helped to straighten him out. He was a deacon in the church now and a model citizen. "I refuse to accept that. It can't be true."

He smiled weakly. "If I ever get in any big trouble, remind me to call you right away, will you? You're a very loyal friend."

"Well, thank you. That's a very nice thing to say, but I'm not defending Odie because I'm loyal. I'm defending him because I truly believe he would never be involved in something like this. Even when he was drinking, he wasn't the type to steal from others. Especially from people in Winter Break. He loves it here."

"I know that. I don't want to believe it either, but what am I supposed to do? I can't ignore this."

I could feel my chest tighten with concern. "What will happen to Odie if you accuse him of stealing from his neighbors? What if he starts drinking again?"

Amos jumped up from his chair, pulling off his hat and smoothing his ash blond hair with his free hand. "You think I haven't thought of that?" He scowled at me. "You act as if you're the only one who's concerned about Odie."

"I never said you didn't care about him. I know you do."

Amos put his hat back on and shook his head. "I'm sorry. I didn't mean to take this out on you."

"That's okay. I understand." I really did. It was easy for me to have an opinion, but I wasn't the one who would have to speak to Odie about it. Amos was under a lot of pressure. "What are you going to do?"

He sat down again. "I'm going to wait as long as I can

before I confront Odie. I've got dates and approximate times that cattle were stolen. Before talking to him, I'll nose around a bit and see if I can't find an alibi for him. If I can prove he was in town, doing something else at the time of the thefts, I'll know he wasn't involved. I won't even bring up his name to the sheriff." Amos stared at me and shrugged. "That's all I can do, Ivy. But if I can't find an alibi. . ." His voice trailed off. He didn't need to finish his sentence. We both knew what would happen. Without warning, Amos clapped his hands together, making me jump. "Now let's change the subject," he said. "Anything interesting happen while I was gone?"

It took a moment for me to respond. I'd been so caught up by Odie's predicament, I'd almost forgotten about the map. "Yes. Which do you want first? The good news or the bad news?"

"There's bad news?" Amos shook his head. "I can't imagine anything worse than what I just told you. . . unless someone died. Did someone die?"

"No. Well, yes, I suppose somewhere in the world someone died, but everyone I know is still breathing."

Amos raised one eyebrow and fixed his incredible amber eyes on me. "You may have noticed that I'm not really in the mood for your twisted humor right now. Why don't you tell me your bad news and get it out of the way."

I took a deep breath. "My parents are on their way to Winter Break. They'll be here Wednesday."

I expected him to commiserate with me, but instead he smiled. "That's not bad news. I'm sure you'll be glad to see them."

"Glad to see them!" I said. "They're coming here for the express purpose of ruining my life. They want me to leave Winter Break."

Amos chuckled. "That's ludicrous. Your parents love you. They'll listen to what you have to say. I think you're letting your imagination run wild."

I held my hand up like a cop stopping traffic. "Wait a minute. You don't really know my parents. You may have met them a few times when we were kids, but you've never spent any *quality* time with them. You have no idea—"

He reached over and grabbed my hand. "I may not know them, but I do know this. God brought us together. *He* says you belong here, with me. Your parents are godly people. They'll recognize His hand in this."

I couldn't think of a response. Amos was going on pure, unadulterated faith, and in my book, and in God's book, nothing on earth was more powerful than that. I felt a sense of relief. Even if I had to cling to Amos's faith alone, at least I could see a life preserver floating in my sea of doubt. It was enough to hold on to for now.

Amos squeezed my hand. "Now what's the good news?"

I felt anticipation build inside me as I pushed the map toward him. "Look what I found hidden inside that old jewelry box Bitty gave me. I think it might be a map to the Lost Gambler's Gold!"

Amos laughed and unfolded the yellowed, brittle paper. "You think George Slocum hid his map in Bitty's jewelry box? That's ridiculous, Ivy. My mom had a jewelry box just like yours. She got it at a carnival. It certainly isn't old enough to belong to Slocum."

I got up and came around the desk so we could look at it together. "Of course I don't think George Slocum put it there. But someone else might have. Someone who was trying to hide it. I mean, what else could it be? As far as I know, there isn't any other treasure around here."

As Amos looked carefully at the details, he shook his head. "This map isn't old enough to belong to George Slocum."

"What are you talking about?" I asked, feeling a rush of indignation. "Of course it is."

"This clearly shows the orchard. Those trees were planted by Harvey Bruenwalder's father in the late forties or early fifties. The orchard didn't exist when George Slocum was alive."

I couldn't argue with him; he was right. My enthusiasm had clouded my judgment. But the flush of disappointment I felt was slowly replaced with a ray of hope as I contemplated the markings on the old piece of paper. "Okay, so it's not a map to Slocum's gold," I said. "But it's a map to something. Something important enough to bury. Maybe this is even bigger than the Gambler's Gold. Maybe—"

Amos's sudden burst of laughter made me jump. "That imagination of yours is something else." He leaned over and kissed me. "It's one of the reasons I love you so much. You're extremely unique."

I smiled at him as sweetly as I could. "Thank you, Amos. I think you're special, too. I also think we should find out what's buried on the far edge of the orchard. I just have a feeling—"

Amos jerked as if he'd been burned. "Oh no. Not again. This never ends well. Somehow I always land knee-deep in trouble when you 'have a feeling.'"

"Well, fine." I sniffed. "I intend to find out what's buried there. With or without you. This map came to me for a reason. It's my destiny to dig it up."

"Your destiny?" Amos shook his head vigorously. "What if this turns out to be something we shouldn't uncover? Has that possibility crossed your mind at all?"

"Nope," I said happily. "I have a feeling this is going to be a good thing. It's too late tonight to go out there, but I'm headed to the orchard tomorrow with a shovel. You can come if you wish. It's totally up to you."

"Do you intend to ask Harvey if it's okay for you to go digging around in his orchard? If I remember right, the last time we did that, he threatened to call the authorities."

I plopped myself on Amos's lap and wrapped my arms around his neck. "But you *are* the authorities, Amos. So if he calls anyone, he'd have to call you. I'd say we're in good shape, wouldn't you?"

"Oh, man. Now I'm the one who has a feeling. And my feeling says that—"

I kissed him before he could finish his sentence.

"Okay, I'll call Harvey and see if he'll let us check this out," he said after I pulled back. He gently pushed me off his lap and stood up. "But I wouldn't count on anything. We're certainly not his favorite people."

Amos headed toward the front door, but before he opened it, he turned around and pointed his finger at me. "Do you promise to stay away from there until I come for you tomorrow afternoon?"

I nodded my head with enthusiasm. "I promise. As long as you get here before it gets late."

"I'll be here by three o'clock. *If* Harvey says it's okay, we'll go to the orchard; then we'll go to Ruby's for dinner, okay?"

I almost jumped with excitement. "Sounds great."

He pulled the door open but turned back once more and frowned at me. "Now, Ivy, I'm willing to dig in one spot and one spot only. If we don't find anything within, say, an hour, we're out of there. Understood?"

"Sure. I've got it."

"I mean it."

"Okay, okay. An hour," I said impatiently. "Now get going. I'll see you tomorrow."

The bell jangled violently as the door slammed behind him. Maybe I hadn't discovered the Lost Gambler's Gold, but something was buried out in the orchard, and we were going to find it. I picked up the map and looked at it again. By tomorrow evening, its secret would be revealed.

Although I'd dismissed his concerns at the time, Amos's words of warning about things that shouldn't be uncovered floated back to me. In fact, they haunted me the rest of evening. Even the TV couldn't distract me completely from an odd sense of foreboding. Around midnight, I turned off the television and fell into a troubled sleep. I dreamed I was walking through the orchard when suddenly a bony hand shot up from underneath the ground and grabbed my ankle. I woke up in a sweat, certain I'd cried out. Miss Skiffins was crouching, staring at me. A peal of thunder added to the frightened cat's panic. I picked her up and comforted her until she began to purr. After she settled down and went back to sleep, I snuggled under the covers and listened to the sound of rain hitting the roof while I contemplated my nightmare. It was similar to the one I'd had as a kid after being told the story of the Gambler's ghost, but there was an obvious difference that made this dream even more frightening.

This time, the person in the orchard wasn't George Slocum. Someone else was buried there.

And he was waiting for me.

4

Tuesday morning dragged by. When Isaac left at two o'clock, I was about ready to jump out of my skin. I could hardly wait to find out what was buried beneath the earth at the edge of the peach grove. The trepidation I'd felt the night before had evaporated like early morning mist in the glow of my unbridled enthusiasm.

By two thirty, I was ready to go, sitting at my desk, gazing out the window. By three o'clock, I was antsy and intently focused on my desk clock's second hand.

By three thirty, I was holding a small shovel and on my way out the door. Amos had promised to meet me by three. He was probably just tied up somewhere, looking for more missing cows. I reassured myself that if Harvey had said we couldn't dig in the orchard, Amos would have called me right away. It sounded okay in my head, and I was so determined to see just what kind of treasure the map would reveal, I didn't allow any other thoughts to interfere with what I wanted to think.

I drove away as quickly as I could without drawing attention to myself, the map lying beside me on the car seat. As I neared the edge of town, I found myself looking around for signs of a familiar patrol car. I'd tried to convince myself that I had nothing to feel guilty about, but the fact that I kept checking for Amos was most likely a good indication that my conscience wasn't completely clear.

"Amos knows where I'm going," I said aloud to no one. "He probably intends to meet me at the grove." When several minutes passed without a lightning strike, I decided to ignore the uncomfortable feeling in the pit of my stomach.

I drove slowly past Harvey's place. His old, battered truck wasn't there, and I didn't see anyone stirring. I pulled onto the dirt road that led to the orchard and parked as far away from Harvey's house as I could. Then with the map in one hand and my shovel in the other, I made my way to the center of the orchard.

I quickly discovered that the odd drawing in the middle of the map was an old campfire pit. Years ago, Harvey and his wife had hosted jamborees for Scout troops from the small towns that surrounded Winter Break. I was too young to have seen this myself, but I'd heard about it. When Harvey's wife took off, he'd shut down the campfires, but I could still see the depression where the pit had been. There were still a few old, rotted logs that lay scattered haphazardly around its edges.

With a few glances around to ensure I was alone, I counted off the steps drawn on the map. There were thirty-one. Since I had no idea who had drawn the map, or how big their steps were, I was at a disadvantage. Thirty-one steps for my short legs might be twenty for someone with a larger stride. However, the tracks seemed to stop at the edge of the orchard. If the tree line was the same, I should be able to approximate it fairly closely.

After one more furtive look around, I stepped forward and started counting. "One, two, three, four, five. . ." When I finally said, "Thirty-one," I stopped and looked down. I was at the edge of the orchard, but was I really in the right spot? Then I noticed something odd sticking out of the ground, near the base of the tree in front of me. I knelt down to look at it for a moment before trying to pull it out. It took several hard tugs to break it free. Although most people would have no idea what it was, I did. It was an old barrel tapper, used to cut holes in barrels of whiskey. Amos and I had found one once when we were kids. Deputy Sheriff Watson noticed us with it and was extremely interested in where we'd discovered it. The only person in Winter Break who would have need of something to tap barrels of booze was Hiram Ledbetter. Always on the lookout for Hiram's still, Morley Watson took off toward the spot by Winter Break Lake where we'd found the barrel tapper lying under the dock. It hadn't done any good; Hiram wasn't anywhere near the lake. The deputy sheriff had hit another dead end.

I gazed down at the tapper, wondering why anyone would stick something like this in the dirt. Then it dawned on me. They were marking the spot. The tapper looked old enough to have been there for a long, long time.

I put it on the ground next to me. I was so excited

I felt as though my insides were doing cartwheels. This was the place. After one more look around, I picked up my shovel and started digging. It was much harder work than I thought it would be. Thank goodness, the ground was soft due to the rain overnight, but the wet dirt was heavy. I carved out a circle about five feet across since I had no idea how close to the old tool the treasure might be.

After about forty minutes, my arms were stiff and sore. At one point, I almost gave up, but my natural nosiness wouldn't allow me to walk away. It took another twenty minutes before the tip of my shovel hit something solid. With growing excitement, I dug around the area a little more and then jumped down into the shallow hole. I brushed some remaining dirt off the top of a rectangular object until I could get my fingers around it and pull it out. It was an old metal box. I felt the hair on the back of my neck stand up. Maybe this really was the Lost Gambler's Gold! Could Amos be wrong about the map?

I brushed the grime off the front of the box the best I could. The metal was crusted with dirt and rust, and I could feel it flaking apart in my hands. I decided to wait and open it under more controlled conditions, but as I stepped out of the hole, I lost my grip and the box tumbled from my hands. The ancient clasp holding it shut broke off on impact, and the box's contents spilled out, tumbling back into the hole.

"Shoot and bother," I grumbled. I knelt down and

picked up each item, placing them gently back into the box. Unfortunately, there wasn't any gold. There were some metal objects, a couple of pictures, and a few other things I didn't bother to look at too closely. I wanted to get my discovery out of the hole, cover up the mess I'd made in Harvey's peach grove, and go someplace where I could have a more leisurely look at the box and its contents.

I'd placed everything I could find back in the decaying container when I realized there was still something lying at the bottom of the hole. I'd almost missed it. It was so corroded I'd mistaken it for a part of the dirt that surrounded it. I got on my knees, reached down, and grabbed it, but it seemed to be caught on something. I pulled a little harder, and it finally came loose, breaking a chain that had been attached. I held it up. It looked like a medal of some kind, but it was hard to tell. It needed to be cleaned. Before I got up, I noticed long, light-colored sticks snaking under the earth, running parallel to each other. They were probably tree roots, although one of them had broken apart when I yanked the medal out of the ground. Roots that dry didn't bode well for the tree they belonged to, but the tree looked perfectly healthy. I stood up and grabbed my shovel. It was heavy with impacted dirt. I hit it several times against the tree to loosen the mud before I realized I'd made several cuts into the trunk. "Oh, phooey," I said out loud. Harvey wasn't going to take kindly to this injury. I touched the grooves with my fingers. They were deep but probably not bad enough to cause any real damage. I noticed that the ruts made an almost perfect *H*. Maybe Harvey would be forgiving since I'd carved his initial into the tree.

Fat chance.

I carried my find carefully to the car. Thankfully, there was an empty paper bag in my trunk that I could put the fragile container in. The clasp was gone, and I didn't want another accident.

It took me awhile to cover up the hole and put the barrel tapper back where I'd found it. By the time I got back to my car, it was almost time to meet Amos at Ruby's. I stopped for a moment at Harvey's, since his truck was still gone, and availed myself of his outdoor water pump. After washing my hands and face and brushing off my clothes the best I could, I'd done everything possible to look presentable. Under normal circumstances, I would never enter a restaurant in my current condition, but in Winter Break, many of the farmers who came in to get a bite of lunch or dinner at Ruby's were still grimy from the fields. I'd probably fit right in.

Besides my obvious unkempt appearance, I was beginning to deal with my similarly soiled conscience. I'd come up with several seemingly valid excuses for my jaunt to Harvey's, but I knew down deep inside that I should have waited for Amos. My overwhelming enthusiasm had drowned out the still, small voice inside me—again. Getting what I wanted sometimes seemed more important than doing what I knew was right. It was one of my greatest weaknesses.

As I neared Ruby's, I kept trying to come up with ways to explain my actions to Amos, but it wasn't working. "I'm sorry, Lord," I said quietly before I got out of the car. "I did it again, didn't I? Please forgive me."

As I pushed open the front door of Ruby's, I was determined to tell Amos the truth, admit my duplicity, and take whatever I deserved. I could only hope that Harvey had said yes to our request. Then Amos wouldn't be quite so upset with me. I looked through the sea of people crowded into wooden booths with red-padded seats and red-checked tablecloths. Finally, I saw him seated at a table in the middle of the room. Great. I'd hoped we'd get one of the booths against the wall. Now I was going to have to confess my sins surrounded by half the population of Winter Break.

Amos looked my way, and I waved at him while giving him one of my most innocent smiles. However, one look at me and the bag in my hands, and Amos's expression changed. He knew what I'd done.

"Ivy Towers," he hissed as I slid into the chair across from him, "I told you to wait for me. What did you do?"

Forgetting my previous good intentions, I automatically went on the defensive. "You promised to pick me up at three," I shot back. "Where were you?"

"Questioning Odie Rimrucker about those stolen cows," Amos said, frowning. "It took a lot longer than I planned."

"What? I thought you weren't going to bother him about it."

Amos's right eyebrow shot up. "You have a very selective memory, you know that? I told you I would try to check out his alibi. If I could confirm that he was somewhere else during the thefts, I'd leave him alone." He sighed, pulled off his hat, and ran his hand across his face. "I asked around. No one could tell me if he was in town during the times the cows went missing."

"I still say Odie wouldn't steal. You know him better than that."

He grunted. "I think I know you, too, Ivy, but then you do something that makes me wonder."

"Look, you told me to wait until three o'clock—"

"Just stop it," he retorted angrily. "You knew I didn't want you going to the orchard by yourself. I made it very clear that—"

"You can stop hollering at me," I said, interrupting what promised to be a long diatribe. "I know I messed up. I should have waited." I reached over and took his hand. "I'm sorry. I really am."

Amos looked like a cat whose canary had just flown away. "Well, I. . .I mean. . ." He frowned at me. "It's no fun when you admit you're wrong, you know," he said. "I have nowhere to go. And I wasn't hollering. I was speaking distinctly."

I risked a small smile. "I don't like it when you 'speak distinctly.' It makes me feel like you're mad at me."

Amos shook his head. "I wasn't able to get in touch with Harvey."

"You mean we didn't have permission to dig in the orchard?"

"No. If you'd waited on me, you'd have learned that."

Now I really felt guilty. "I guess I'll have to go to him and admit what I did, won't I?" I asked the question hoping Amos would come up with some reason I should keep the incident to myself. He didn't.

"Yes, you're going to tell him. And right away. In fact, I want you to go over to Harvey's either tonight or first thing in the morning."

I knew there was no point in arguing. Amos was as stubborn as I was. When he made up his mind, it was useless to try to change it.

"Amos," I said, hoping my transgressions hadn't completely ruined the excitement of my discovery, "I found a box buried right where the map said it would be."

Before he had a chance to respond, Bonnie Peavey, Ruby's longtime waitress, stepped up to our booth. "Whatcha havin'?" she asked in a quiet voice.

Bonnie had lived in Winter Break her entire life. Her parents, along with her two brothers and twin sister, still lived on the original family homestead. One of her brothers, Earl, lived in the same house as her parents, while Connie and Billy Ray, her younger brother, had their own houses built on Peavey land. Bonnie, the renegade of the bunch, rented a room at Sarah Johnson's. She always seemed rather lonely, and I felt sorry for her.

After Amos and I had ordered and Bonnie had strolled away, I set the sack on the table.

"I don't know if we should be looking at this, Ivy," Amos said. "This is actually Harvey's property. Maybe it's too late to put it back, but I don't think I'm comfortable with going through it unless Harvey knows about it."

"I've already seen what's inside," I said, "so that horse has left the barn. After I explain everything to Harvey, if he wants the box back, we'll give it to him. I just want one close look at the contents; then I'll be satisfied."

Amos seemed to consider this for a moment. I could tell he was just as curious as I was. "Okay," he said finally. "One good look—then we turn the box and the contents over to Harvey. Agreed?"

I nodded so vigorously, I almost gave myself a headache. I slowly pulled the box out of the bag and set it on top of the sack so it wouldn't mess up Ruby's clean table.

Amos picked up his napkin and started wiping off the top of the container. Although the paint was faded and sections were eaten away by rust, a picture began to emerge. He peered closely at the place he'd cleared and frowned. He wiped a little more then set his napkin down and started to chuckle.

"What's so funny?" I asked, feeling a little offended.

He shook his head. "Oh dear. I almost hate to tell you this."

"What? What is it?"

Amos started to laugh again, and I reached out for the container, determined to see for myself just what it was that was so humorous.

Amos pushed it toward me. "You have certainly uncovered a very valuable treasure," he sputtered, his face red with exertion. "Ivy Towers, you have unearthed an actual Bonanza lunch box!"

"A what?" Sure enough, peering back from the top of the box were Hoss and Ben Cartright. I was pretty sure the green-shirted arm to their right was Little Joe. Well, unless the Lost Gambler was a lot more contemporary than the stories suggested, this hadn't belonged to him at all. Amos snorted as he launched into another round of giggles.

I glared at him in an attempt to shut him up. People were beginning to stare. I decided to ignore him and carefully removed the cover and set it down next to the box. I unrolled the napkin that held my silverware and laid it out on the table. One by one, I began taking items from the box. Although they were obviously old, most of them were in pretty good shape. There was also a piece of aluminum foil that must have been wrapped around the objects until I'd dropped them into the hole.

Amos finally settled down, and although our previous level of enthusiasm had leveled off quite a bit, looking at items that had meant so much to someone so long ago was still extremely interesting. He leaned over to watch me as I carefully removed each object and gently put them on my napkin.

"These look like some kind of medals," I said.

Amos took them from me and turned them over in his hand. "They're track medals," he said. "Whoever they belonged to was pretty good, I'd say."

He put them on the napkin as I lifted out an old knife. Amos grabbed that from me also.

"It's an old Boy Scout knife," he said. "Odie has one just like it. I guess he used to belong to a Scout troop here in Winter Break when he was a kid. Dewey was the scoutmaster."

"Dewey?" I was surprised. I thought I knew everything about Dewey Tater, but I didn't remember ever hearing this before.

"What else is in there?" Amos asked, his interest obviously piqued.

"There are some pictures," I said. "Maybe they'll give us a clue as to who owns this lunch box."

One of the photographs was of a man standing next to a tractor. The other picture showed a beautiful young girl. She was holding something, but the picture was too faded for me to see what it was. The background made me think of a country fair. All the photographs were in remarkably good shape except for a little fading and something that looked like mold around the edges. But no one in the pictures looked the least bit familiar.

"Is that everything?" Amos asked.

"No, there's a small Bible here." As I lifted the Bible out of the box, the cover began flaking apart in my hands. A small, dried flower that had been pressed between the pages fell out onto the table.

Amos carefully picked up the flower and put it on the napkin. "Look at the front pages and see if anyone's name is written inside."

Before I had a chance to open the cover, I heard a gasp from behind me. I turned to see Ruby Bird looking over my shoulder, her face drained of color, her eyes wide. Thankfully, Amos jumped up just in time to catch her before she fainted.

5

Any chance of keeping our discovery quiet disappeared with Ruby's strange reaction to seeing the lunch box and the things inside it sprawled out across our table. We had quite a crowd gathered around, and everyone wanted to know where the box had come from and to whom it belonged. My search for secret treasure had turned into a group event. Making things even worse, Harvey Bruenwalder walked in the door right after Ruby's fainting spell. My hope of confessing my sins in private disappeared like smoke in the wind.

"Everybody move back and give Ruby some room," Amos barked to the throng of people leaning over to see what was going on. Reluctantly, several Winter Break folks took a step backward, but everyone seemed determined to stay within hearing distance.

I looked around me. It seemed as if half the town was in Ruby's. I saw Elmer Buskins, the funeral director, and Isaac was standing next to Alma Pettibone. Standing off a bit from the crowd was Odie Rimrucker. His gaze was locked on Amos, and his expression was anything but happy. I felt someone touch my shoulder.

"Ivy, what's going on? Is there anything I can do to help?"

I turned to see Pastor Taylor and his wife at the table behind us. My old childhood friend Emily Taylor and her husband, Buddy, the pastor's son, were sitting with them. Emily smiled at me, and I smiled back. "Maybe so, Pastor," I said. "Could you check to see if Ruby is okay? I think she fainted, and I—"

"Ivy Towers!"

Ruby's loud voice cut through the air, stopping any further conversation. "Where in the world did you get this?"

The restaurant owner was obviously feeling better. Her hearing problems raised her voice several decibels above normal human tones. I began to wonder if I shouldn't just stand up on the table and shout out the whole situation.

Ruby straightened her Marilyn Monroe–styled wig, which was now slightly askew, and gazed down at the contents of the box. Amos had helped her into the chair next to him right before she tried to hit the ground. Since he was surrounded by curious onlookers, he was now a prisoner. And he wasn't happy about it. I glanced over at him, hoping he would field Ruby's question. He gave me a look that could freeze molten · lava. I was definitely on my own.

"It was buried in the peach grove, Ruby," I said, trying not to look at Harvey. "I went there because I found this." I pulled the map out of my purse and handed it to her. Ruby unfolded it and started to cry. All around us, I could hear people whispering to one another.

"She found it where?"

"What is it?"

"What'd she say, Bertha? What'd she say?"

I recognized Marybelle Widdle's voice. Great. She was here with Bertha Pennypacker. They went everywhere together. Bertha had it in for me. I had no idea why, but the woman detested me. No matter what I said to her, or how I tried to befriend her, she would always defeat my attempts with an icy stare or a snide comment. This was going to give her a lot of fuel for her "I hate Ivy" fire.

I noticed Harvey Bruenwalder standing behind Elmer. His fierce expression made it clear that I was going to have a lot of explaining to do. He didn't say anything, and this wasn't the time for me to talk to him about my transgression. But I was aware that I would certainly have to mend my fences with him as soon as possible.

Trying to ignore the sick feeling in my stomach, I turned my attention away from our audience and tried to concentrate on Ruby. Reaching across the table, I let my fingers lightly touch her arm. "Ruby, what is it? Who does this belong to?"

Without answering me, she put the map down on the table and lifted the moldy cover of the little Bible. Still visible, although it was faded and had traces of mildew, was a scrawled signature: *Bert Bird.*

Bert Bird? Ruby's son? I'd heard stories about him when I was a kid. About how he'd left town when he was a teenager and never come back.

"This was my boy's lunch pail," Ruby said loudly

enough for everyone to hear. "And these are his track medals. This is his Bible." She picked up one of the pictures. As she gazed at the man on the tractor, she began to cry harder. "My husband, Elbert," she croaked through her sobs. "This was taken a couple of months before he died. That's me standing next to him."

I took the picture from her trembling fingers. I hadn't noticed the wisp of a woman standing beside the tractor. If I had, I doubt I would have recognized her. Ruby's dark, expressive eyes were wide and innocent, and her face was framed by thick ebony hair plaited into a long braid that fell over her shoulder. Her shy smile and delicate features reminded me of a gentle fawn. This woman was a far cry from the tough, leather-skinned Ruby of today. As I looked a little closer, I could finally see the similarities in her features. The hair was what really threw me, since I'd never actually seen Ruby's hair.

Amos handed her his handkerchief, which she gratefully accepted. After she wiped her eyes and took a few deep breaths, she picked up the second picture.

"Oh my goodness," she said.

"What is it, Ruby?" I asked as softly as I dared. Ruby's hearing problems didn't allow for a lot of subtlety.

"Bonnie! Bonnie Peavey!" Ruby suddenly screeched.

Poor Bonnie jumped as if someone had plugged her into an electric outlet. One look at the picture made her turn as white as Ruby had moments earlier. I wasn't worried about Bonnie falling to the floor, since there were so many people gathered around her. If she passed out, the worst that could happen was that she would end up leaning a little to the left.

"Bonnie Peavey!" Ruby squealed again. "What is your picture doing in my son's lunch box?"

Now all eyes were focused on the hapless waitress. Her usually somber features were alive with emotion. "I. . .I. . .I don't know. That was thirty years ago, Ruby," she said softly. Too softly for the crowd trying to figure out what was going on.

"What did she say?" Bertha Pennypacker said in her eternally whiny voice. "I can't hear her."

"Something about the picture bein' dirty," a raspy male voice said. "Move over, Elmer. I can't see it."

"She said *thirty*, not *dirty*," Elmer Buskins squeaked. Of course, with his speech impediment, it actually came out, "*tirty*, not *dirty*."

"Huh?" someone else said. "What was that?"

I'd had enough. I managed to wiggle out of my chair. Then I pushed a few people back so I could get some breathing room. "Would all of you please go back to your seats and let us talk to Ruby? If anything important comes up, we'll make sure you all know about it."

"And just how do you propose to do that?" Bertha Pennypacker asked icily.

"Why don't you just tell it to Alma Pettibone?" someone asked with a snicker.

I looked over at Alma. She flushed beet red and began

to fight her way through the crowd, most probably heading toward the front door. Isaac turned to watch her leave and then followed after her. Good. His compassionate nature would help to soothe her hurt feelings.

"I mean it, everyone," I said with a little more force. "Go sit down. Give Ruby a little space."

Of course, no one moved. I was trying to come up with something a little more threatening when Amos stood up and addressed the crowd.

"Now listen here, folks," he said in his down-home, unthreatening style, "I know you all care very much about Ruby and just want to help her. For right now, the best thing you can do is to give her a little space so she can look over her son's possessions. Let's give her some respect and peace. In a few days, I'm sure Ruby will be more than happy to share her feelings with you. But not right now, okay?"

Some people began moving, but several just glared at Amos and stood their ground. Just then, Dewey Tater made his way through the crowd. "You heard Amos," he said loudly. "You people start minding your own business. This is Ruby's business. Let's leave her to it."

As if Dewey were the pied piper himself, the rest of the rats turned and scattered back to their respective holes. Their reaction made it clear why Dewey was the mayor. The fact that I compared the good citizens of Winter Break to rats made it obvious I wasn't cut out for political office.

Once the crowd had dispersed, the only people near Ruby were Dewey, Amos, and me. Dewey started to walk away, but Ruby grabbed his arm and asked him to stay.

At first Ruby was silent, turning each item over in her fingers, gazing at it longingly. She picked up the medal that was the most dirt encrusted and stared at it for a moment. "I don't recognize this," she said finally. "Maybe if it was cleaned up some."

"I'll scrub it for you, Ruby," I said. "In fact, I'll clean everything up as much as I can." Aunt Bitty had used saddle soap to clean the covers of some of the old leather-bound books in her collection. Bert's Bible might be beyond that stage, but I could contact some other rare book dealers for advice. Amos could help with the rusty medals. I wanted to give Ruby back her newfound treasures in better shape than they were in now.

"Thank you, Ivy," the old woman said. "Why don't you take the box and bring it back when you're done? I don't think I can look at this stuff any more right now."

Her thin fingers slowly closed the lid on the fragile lunch box. I was pretty sure it wasn't going to make it through any kind of cleanup. It was in pretty bad shape, but I didn't want to bring that up now.

Ruby reached over and patted the chair next to her, motioning Dewey to sit down, which he did.

Pastor Taylor stood up and came over to us. "Ruby, we're going to take our food to another table. We don't want to intrude on a private conversation—"

"No, no, Pastor," Ruby said. "I wish you would stay. It would comfort me."

Pastor Taylor nodded and sat back down. He turned his chair slightly so Ruby could see him; then he smiled at her. "So these things belonged to your son, Bert? I don't know much about him, Ruby, since we weren't in Winter Break yet when he left. Would you like to tell us a little about him?"

I smiled appreciatively at him. His soft-spoken, caring style was just what Ruby needed. She looked up, tears streaming down her weather-beaten face as if they had a life of their own. "Bert was a wonderful boy," she said. "He always helped out on the farm, glad to do anything he could to help his daddy. He was the joy of my life, always tryin' to make me laugh. And he loved my cookin'. In fact, he was the one who used to tell me I could open a restaurant. When I sold the farm, I opened the diner because of him." She stopped. Amos offered her his handkerchief, and she wiped her face with it.

"I never knew that, Ruby," Dewey said.

She shook her head slowly. "I don't think I ever told anyone." She stared at him for a moment, her eyes shiny with tears. "You remember Bert, don't you, Dewey? You were his scoutmaster. In fact, I think you gave him this Boy Scout knife."

"Yes, I did. And of course I remember him," Dewey said gently. "He was a fine boy. One of the best boys I ever worked with."

Ruby nodded. "Yes, he really was a wonderful young man. But after his daddy died so unexpectedly, he began to change. He was angry, I think. Angry at God. Angry at me. I don't know." She paused and blew her nose.

I doubted Amos was going to want that handkerchief back.

"It was too much for him," she continued. "Tryin' to be a boy and a man at the same time. It was too much to ask. I shouldn't have put him in that position."

"Nonsense," Dewey said. "It wasn't your fault. You were trying to keep the farm afloat."

"Is that why he left, Ruby?" I asked.

Ruby stiffened as if someone had thrown cold water into her face.

"I sent him to stay with relatives," she said icily. "He just never came back." She shoved the box toward me. "I'd appreciate it if you would clean this up. I'd like to have Bert's stuff as mementos. I guess he buried it sometime before he left and forgot about it." She turned and hollered at poor Bonnie, who was taking orders at a nearby table. "Maybe when we close up tonight, Bonnie, you can explain to me why your picture is in my son's lunch box."

Bonnie's eyes widened, and she scampered off toward the kitchen. I was pretty interested in the answer to that question. Had Bert and Bonnie dated? They would have been rather young.

Ruby stood up and faced us. "I want to thank you

all for listenin' to me. I know you care, and that means a lot. This discovery shook me up some, I admit that. But Bert is gone, and I don't think he's ever comin' back. I will treasure these things you found, Ivy. Thank you. But it's time to go on with life. I can't live in the past. There's just no purpose in it."

With that, she turned on her heel and headed toward the kitchen. The quiet atmosphere in the diner, the result of people trying to listen in on our conversation, exploded with voices, everyone talking about the strange situation we'd just encountered. Bonnie scurried away behind Ruby.

"I'm sorry," I said to Amos and Dewey. "I should have kept my mouth shut. I had no idea she would close up like that."

"It's not you, Ivy," Dewey said. "She's been like that ever since Bert left. A lot of people have tried to talk to her about it, but she just clams up."

"Why would she do that?" someone said behind me. I'd forgotten about Pastor Taylor and jumped at the sound of his voice.

"It doesn't make sense," I said. "If Bert went to stay with relatives while Ruby straightened out her problems with the farm, why didn't he come back? There's obviously something Ruby doesn't want to tell anyone."

"I imagine it's just too painful for her to discuss," Dewey said. "I'm sure it's very difficult to admit that your own flesh and blood decided to live with someone else. Ruby's never gotten over it."

Though I didn't respond to Dewey's remark, I wasn't sure I agreed with him. Ruby's abrupt change of attitude smacked of some kind of secret. What happened next only deepened my conviction that there was a mystery of some kind lurking beneath the disappearance of Bert Bird.

"Where's the map?" I asked, noticing that it was gone. We looked under the napkins and on the floor, but it was nowhere to be found. Had Ruby taken it? The only thing I'd seen clutched in her hands when she left was Amos's handkerchief. And if she didn't have the map, who did? And why?

B ut that doesn't make any sense," I told Amos as we sat together on the front porch of the bookstore. I'd purchased a pair of white rocking chairs in Hugoton so that Amos and I could sit outside and watch the town come alive with spring colors and smells. The cicadas supplied our background music. Their throbbing cadence at dusk was irritating to some, but I found it incredibly soothing. The throaty contralto voices sang backup to the many birds that made Winter Break their home. In my mind, cicadas were the harbingers of spring and the oft-maligned troubadours of summer.

"You're reading too much into this, Ivy," he said gruffly. "You think there's a mystery behind everything unusual that happens. The map probably fell on the floor, and someone picked it up and threw it away, thinking it was trash."

I took a deep breath and mentally counted to five. "So the treasure map that led us to finding Bert's possessions, clearly marked with the words *My Treasure*, the same map that created so much interest in the diner, suddenly got confused with garbage?"

I could hear a note of hysteria in my voice, but I was frustrated. Amos was a sheriff's deputy. It seemed to me that he should be able to see that the theft of the map was extremely suspicious.

He sighed and rocked a little harder, a sure sign I was getting on his nerves. "Yes, I think it's possible, Ivy. There's no earthly reason anyone would want that map. Bert's box has already been dug up—thanks to you. The map is worthless now. Meaningless. The only person who might want it would be Ruby. Maybe she took it. After all, her son drew it."

"But why wouldn't she say something about it? Why would she hide it under your handkerchief?"

"Maybe she wasn't trying to hide it at all. Maybe the handkerchief just covered it up. I think you need to leave it alone. You sure can't ask her for it. It isn't yours."

I didn't have an answer for that. He was right. I changed the subject. "What do you know about Bert Bird's disappearance?"

Amos's rocking slowed a little, and in the fading light, I could see his forehead wrinkle. "I've heard a lot of different things. Most of it seems to line up with Ruby's story. Trying to be the man of the house was too much for a sixteen-year-old boy. He went to stay with relatives and just never came back."

"You said 'most' of it lined up with Ruby's story. What do you mean? Do you know something you're not telling me?"

Amos stopped rocking and sighed. "I hesitate to tell you this because of your overactive imagination, but now that I've thought about it, I do remember a conversation I overheard when I was a kid. Morley

Watson and Dewey were talking about Bert's leaving, and Morley said something really odd."

I waited while Amos resumed rocking and staring at the sunset. After what seemed like an eternity, I said, "Would you like to share it with me, or do you want me to try to read your mind?"

"Oh, sorry. I was just thinking about Odie."

I couldn't keep the exasperation out of my voice. "Will you please tell me what Morley said about Bert? We'll have to worry about Odie later. I can only handle one problem at a time."

Amos looked surprised by the impatience in my voice. He was used to living in a small town where everything moved like molasses in the Arctic. I still had big-city blood flowing in my veins. Patience was not so much a virtue as it was an inconvenience.

Amos stopped rocking again. "Well, Ruby kept saying that Bert would be back, but after a while, when he never showed up, I guess they got a little suspicious."

"What do you mean by 'suspicious'?"

"I mean Morley and Dewey wondered if something had happened to Bert. If maybe someone had done something to him."

"What do you mean, 'done something to him'?"

Amos turned and looked at me. "Are you going to keep asking me what I mean?"

I ignored him. "You mean they wondered if Bert was dead?"

He nodded. "Dewey asked Morley if he'd ever

suspected that someone had killed Bert."

I couldn't believe what I was hearing. "What did Deputy Watson say?"

Amos shrugged. "He said he didn't have any evidence of it, but he thought the whole thing was pretty strange. Then he asked Dewey if he'd ever suspected Ruby of being the kind of person who might do away with her son. Dewey said he didn't know her well enough to hazard a guess."

"Amos Parker, why didn't you ever tell me about this? You used to tell me everything when we were kids."

Amos zipped up his jacket and gazed off into the horizon. "At the time, I think it was because it scared me a little. This happened right before my mother married Truman McAlister and took off for California. We weren't getting along, and I felt like I was in her way. I hadn't thought about this for years. Not until today."

I scooted my rocking chair closer to him and grabbed his arm. "Your mother loved you, Amos. She just got caught up with Truman and thought she'd find some kind of happiness with him."

He nodded. "I know. I've made peace with it. We talked several times before she died. I flew out to see her just a month before she passed away. I think we put the past to rest."

"Someday you'll have to do the same with your father," I said softly.

"Let's get back to Bert, okay?" Amos's tone was harsh. His father was still a forbidden subject between us. I wasn't sure why, but I was willing to wait until he was ready to open up. I could sense that pushing him would only make him more defensive.

"Okay. I'm sorry."

We rocked silently for a while. I was turning over the idea of Ruby's being involved in Bert's disappearance, but I just couldn't see it. I didn't pretend to know Ruby that well, but I'd always had a sense about people. My gut told me that Ruby truly loved her son and missed him. But I still couldn't understand why Bert had never come back after all these years. Even it he'd chosen to grow up somewhere else, why hadn't he visited his mother when he was older? And why was Ruby so defensive about it? It just didn't add up.

"I wonder if Ruby even knows where Bert is," I said. "It's obvious she's heartbroken that he's never come back."

"Let it go, Ivy," Amos said. "Once you clean Bert's stuff up and give everything to Ruby, you'll have to walk away and leave her with her memories. That's all she has now. Besides, you need to be thinking about Harvey."

I put my head on Amos's shoulder. "Couldn't you talk to him? He'd accept it better coming from—"

"No," he said, interrupting my heartfelt plea. "You need to do this yourself. You caused this mess. Now you clean it up."

"But, Amos—"

"Don't 'but, Amos' me. You knew I didn't want you going there without me. Your curiosity got out of control again."

"I know, I know." I snuggled up as close as I could to him with the arms of the rocking chairs between us. "I take full responsibility. I'll see Harvey first thing in the morning."

"What time are your parents supposed to get here?" he asked, his tone a little gentler.

"Your guess is as good as mine. I'll drive over to Harvey's first thing in the morning and plan to be back here no later than eleven. They're traveling all the way from Wichita. That's about a six-hour trip. Even if they left at six in the morning, they couldn't be here until noon."

"Do you really think they'd leave that early?"

I laughed. "You really don't know my mother at all, do you? She'd leave even earlier if my dad would let her. And because she's on her way here to 'save me,' she won't waste a minute of her time. She's a very determined woman."

"Well, so are you, Ivy," Amos said. "And together, we're unbeatable."

"Yes, we are," I said as I reached over to accept his kiss.

"I'll pick you up at nine thirty in the morning. We'll visit Harvey together."

I kissed him again and then went inside before he could change his mind. I felt better knowing he would be by my side when I confessed my lack of judgment to Harvey Bruenwalder. Harvey struck me as an eternally grumpy man. I had no idea how he'd take my apology. Unfortunately, Amos and I had been a thorn in his side ever since we were kids. Everyone had their limits.

From the doorway, I watched as Amos's taillights disappeared around the corner. After I shut the door, I went over to my desk where the rusting box sat on a towel. I slowly pulled back the top while the hinges creaked with resistance.

I held the pictures in the desk lamp's light and looked closely at the faces that stared back at me. Elbert Bird had a kind face, with deep-set, dark eyes that suggested a sense of humor. He had the kind of smile that could come only from a man who was truly happy, who had almost everything he wanted in life. Ruby's expression was full of hope, with no doubt of the future before them. I remembered Ruby saying that shortly after this picture was taken, Elbert was killed. I was sad for him, for Ruby, and for Bert.

I put that picture back and picked up the photograph of Bonnie Peavey. If someone hadn't told me who it was, I never would have known. The Bonnie I knew was a shadow of the vibrant young girl with the dazzling smile. Bonnie had been a waitress at Ruby's for as long as I could remember. She was the kind of person who seemed to melt into her surroundings, like a chair or a table. She was there, yet she wasn't. Had Bert's departure robbed her of her vivacity? The girl staring back at me was happy. Her expression went beyond having her picture taken, as if her smile was intended for the person behind the camera. Was it Bert? I couldn't know for sure, but in my heart, I believed it was. Maybe Bonnie had lost the love of her life thirty years ago. Of course, Amos would probably tell me that my imagination was running away with me again, but I wasn't so sure.

I grabbed a sewing box I'd found in Aunt Bitty's room and began putting the items from the lunch box inside it. Bert's friends from the Ponderosa weren't long for this world. His treasures needed a new home.

I set the photographs aside while I carefully fingered each of the medals. The only one that would be hard to clean was the oddly shaped one that had been snagged on tree roots. I couldn't understand why it was so dirty when the other medals were corroded but clean. It was almost as if it had been placed in the box already crusted with dirt and grime. But why would Bert do that?

I was beginning to feel sleepy, and tomorrow was going to be a big day. My parents' arrival would most probably turn my semi-orderly world into chaos. There was a part of me that looked forward to seeing them again—especially my dad. It had been almost two years since I'd had one of his wonderful hugs. My mother was the real problem. Why couldn't I ever seem to please her? My prayer was that she would see how happy I was then go back to China at peace with my choices.

Of course, I also had hopes of someday waking up and finding that I had supernaturally been given a voice like Céline Dion's and a face like Julia Roberts's. So far, that hadn't happened either.

I closed the box and rounded up Miss Skiffins. We

hit the mattress around midnight. It was a little after 3:00 a.m. when I woke up with a start. The tiny cat was digging her claws into my arm with a death grip. As I grabbed her and shook her loose, I realized I could smell smoke. I reached over and clicked on the lamp next to my bed. Miss Skiffins stared at me, her eyes wide with terror. I tucked her under my arm and ran into the hallway. I could see smoke downstairs. I was really thankful that my room had no door, or I might have assumed the cat was having a bad dream and gone back to sleep. For a moment, I hesitated, wondering if I should try to climb out an upstairs window. I looked down at my sweat suit. It was heavy enough, but my feet were bare. While trying to control the struggling feline under my arm, I quickly shoved my feet into my sneakers. Just then, Isaac called my name.

"Ivy! Are you up there?"

"I'm here, Isaac. Is it safe to come downstairs?"

"Yes!" he yelled. "But hurry!"

I ran down the stairs. He was waiting at the bottom. "How bad is it?"

"It's just in the corner by your desk," he said, coughing.

I could see the fire now. It was moving up the wall near the front windows. "We've got to call Milton!"

Isaac was guiding me to the back of the store. "I already called him, Miss Ivy," he said. "He'll be here any minute. You go around front. I'm going to get the fire extinguisher and see if I can't stop this from getting any worse."

"Be careful, Isaac," I yelled as he ran back inside. I tromped around the side of the bookstore. Miss Skiffins was fighting me for all she was worth. Thankfully, my car was unlocked, so I put her inside. I didn't want to drop her and have her run away.

I watched the street in front of the bookstore for the fire department truck. Milton Baumgartner ran the volunteer fire department in Winter Break. We had only one old engine, but the volunteers had protected many a building from destruction in the tiny town.

Within a couple of minutes, I saw the out-of-date, dusty red engine pulling up. Milton was driving. His wife, Mavis, sat next to him in the front seat while their two sons hung on to the sides of the vehicle for dear life. As the Baumgartners piled out, Dewey came running out of his store, still buttoning his shirt. I was glad he lived close by. His presence gave me some reassurance. I knew he would do everything he could to save the bookstore.

Almost immediately, Mavis began barking out orders to her family. She was a large woman with bright lemon yellow hair piled precariously on top of her head. Mavis Baumgartner was a force to be reckoned with, and she ran her family like a drill sergeant cursed with an unruly command. Although all our volunteers had been given firefighters' outfits by the Stevens County Fire Department, only the men had them on. Mavis was so massive she couldn't fit into hers. Instead, she wore a big, bright yellow rain poncho over her long flannel nightgown. As she clomped around in enormous black rubber boots, with her poncho flapping in the breeze and her overly bleached bun beginning to come loose from the hairpins that were trying valiantly to keep it secure, she looked like Big Bird with an attitude and a bad dye job.

Before long, other people started showing up. It was the nature of a small town. When one person was in trouble, everyone joined in to help. I felt someone grab my arm. It was Amos.

"Ivy! What happened?"

I fell back into his arms. "I. . .I don't know. I was sleeping. Isaac got us out."

Isaac. I turned to find him, but he was helping the Baumgartners get the hose from the truck. Our fire truck was a tanker truck, which meant it had water inside. Of course, this made the engine heavy and rather slow, but since the fire station was only six blocks away, it hadn't cost us much time. However, if they couldn't put out the fire with the water they had, there would be a big problem. Although Winter Break had a few fire hydrants, the bookstore was almost two blocks away from one. I prayed that the water they had would be enough.

Amos ran over to help with the hose. When the water gushed out, it took only a few minutes for the fire to fizzle and die out. By the time it was over, thankfully, I could see that only one corner of the store was affected. With Miss Skiffins finally calmed down some in the backseat of my car, Amos and I went inside to survey the damage. It seemed to be confined to the area near my desk. Aunt Bitty's antique desk was ruined, as was her chair and the portion of the room that surrounded it.

Isaac walked up behind me. "Thank God the books are all right," he said. "But are the records gone? All our work. . ."

I turned around and hugged him. Isaac had never been very touchy-feely before, but he hugged me back, not seeming to have a problem with our sudden bout of intimacy.

"Thankfully, I've been working on the books in the sitting room and didn't put them back in the desk. They're fine. But even more important than that," I said earnestly, "thank you for getting Miss Skiffins and me out of there."

He smiled in the dusky room, illuminated only by the fire engine's headlights. "I had no choice. You pay my salary."

I ignored his attempt to lighten the situation. "I mean it, Isaac."

"It could have been much worse," he said. "The fire was still small enough so that I could get most of it under control with the extinguisher. Thankfully, I smelled the smoke when I got up to get some milk because I couldn't sleep. It's a good thing my apartment is right next door."

"And it's a good thing you picked tonight to have insomnia."

Amos slapped Isaac on the back. "It doesn't matter how large the fire was, Isaac. You handled it like a pro. Good job."

Even in the semidarkness, I could see Isaac blush. "Well, be that as it may, Deputy, I am still concerned about our books. I wonder if the smoke will affect them."

Mavis came clomping up to us. "The fire was contained to this one area, and most of the smoke drifted toward the door and windows. You're going to have to do some cleanup, but my guess is that you'll find most of your books in fine shape. You really caught it early. All in all, things turned out as well as could be expected." She shone her flashlight at the wall behind us. "Looks like it started right here." The beam of light focused on a charred outlet in the wall.

"Must have been an electrical problem," I said.

Mavis stomped over to the switch and then knelt down and put her nose next to it. She shook her head and stood up slowly. "You smell something?" she asked Amos.

Amos leaned down and sniffed. "Gasoline?"

Mavis nodded vigorously, her hair flying frantically around her head.

"What are you saying?" I asked. "Someone. . . someone set this fire on purpose?"

"We can't be sure of that, Ivy," Amos said. "But it certainly looks suspicious."

"But why?"

Mavis and Amos just looked at me. Isaac shook his head sadly. I was flabbergasted. Who in the world would want to burn the bookstore—with me in it?

"Whoever did this had to know I was here," I said slowly. "Could they have been trying to hurt me?"

"If someone had wanted to hurt you, Ivy," Mavis said kindly, "I think they would have tried starting the fire somewhere else. Seems to me like their goal was the building." She studied the burned fixture for a moment. "I think someone wanted us to think a short circuit started the blaze." She smiled at me. "Sorry I can't tell you more. This isn't *CSI*. It's just Winter Break. Our job is to put out fires. I don't know much about arson. Only remember one arson fire. Ben Willard thought he could get some insurance money for burning down his barn. Silly fool used so much gasoline he lost his house and his tractor to boot." She shook her head. "At least all you've got is minor damage. I guess we can be thankful for that."

Mavis might know how to put out a fire, but she sure didn't understand what "minor damage" was. Aunt Bitty's beautiful desk and antique chair were gone. That wasn't minor to me. However, I was grateful the whole store hadn't gone up in flames.

Just then, one of Mavis's boys came around the corner. "Think everything's under control, Ma. We wet down the outside real good. This fire shouldn't be startin' up again."

"Thanks, Pervis," she said.

"You need to find somewhere else to stay," Mavis said. "We smashed your door in, and it's gonna stink in here for a while. It'd be best if you could go somewhere for a few days while things get repaired."

Amos put his arm around me. "She's right, Ivy. Why don't you go upstairs and grab a few things? I'll take you somewhere else for tonight at least."

I pulled away from him. "I don't want to go, Amos. This is my home. Besides, I'll be upstairs. I'll be okay."

Mavis shook her head. "That's the worst place you could be. Even though we've drenched this area, we can't guarantee it won't flare up again. You can't be here until we're absolutely sure it's safe."

"How could someone get in, Mavis? I'm sure the door was locked."

Using her grime-encrusted hand, she reached up to stabilize her quickly disintegrating bun. "Can't really tell, honey. Maybe someone jimmied the lock. Could be they just kicked it in. It's also possible you just thought the door was locked. That was a pretty door, but it sure wasn't very durable." She put her hand on my shoulder. "It won't take us long to clean this up. We'll have things as good as new before you know it. I'll make sure you get a door that's pretty *and* strong, okay?"

"She's right, Ivy," Milton said from behind me. I turned around to see his sons nodding their agreement.

"But. . .but it isn't your job to fix this," I said, waving my hand toward the blackened furniture and the wall behind it.

"You know better than that," Dewey said as he came toward us. "Folks in Winter Break see themselves as family. What hurts you hurts all of us. You get your stuff and stay away for a few days. I'll keep an eye on things. We'll start the cleanup tomorrow. First thing you know, you'll be back in business."

"Thank you," I sputtered, feeling overwhelmed by the generosity being shown to me. "Thank you, everyone. But, Amos, where will I stay? Sarah Johnson is full up. I can't think of any other place."

I knew Dewey would have asked me to stay with him, but his apartment above the store was as tiny as mine. There wasn't room.

"I have an idea," Amos said. "You just go and pack. Everything will be okay."

I started toward the stairs when I remembered something. "Oh no! Amos, I had Bert's lunch box on the desk!"

I hurried over to the charred remains of the desk. Mavis shone her flashlight over the surface. Everything was there, including my ruined laptop, the charred desk lamp, the blackened pencil holder, the melted stapler, and my overly cooked phone.

But Bert Bird's lunch box and personal treasures were gone.

You can't ignore this, Amos," I said after he shuffled me into his patrol car. "Whoever tried to burn down the bookstore was after Bert's lunch box. There is something nefarious going on here, and we have to figure out what it is!"

"Nefarious?" Amos said. "Why do you have to talk like that? Who uses words like *nefarious*?"

"I do, that's who," I snapped. I wanted immediate action. It seemed to me that Amos was so wrapped up in small-town reticence, it was going to take forever to get things moving. "What's your plan? Wait until someone is dead and then take this whole thing seriously?"

Amos pulled the car over. "Ivy," he said, twisting in his seat so he could properly glare at me. "I'm not an idiot, although you act like I am. I dragged you away because you can't keep your mouth shut. Your curiosity about Bert was one thing. I could even overlook the map's disappearance, but the fire and the theft of Bert's things? There is obviously something going on here. I'd like a chance to find out what it is, but it's going to be tough if you're busy telling everybody and their neighbor that we're suspicious."

"Oh." I patted his arm. "I'm sorry. I should have known better. At least the only people who could have overheard me were people we can trust." I blinked back an attack of pesky tears. "I guess I'm just emotional about the bookstore. Aunt Bitty expected me to take care of it. I didn't do a very good job."

Amos reached over and took my chin in his hand. His hazel eyes locked onto mine. "You listen here. This wasn't your fault at all. We're going to figure out what's going on, and we're going to get the bookstore back up on its feet. Don't worry about it, okay?"

I nodded. Then I reached over and kissed him. "Okay. I won't. But this is really going to give my mother something to rant about. How am I going to explain it?"

Amos let go of my face and leaned back in his seat. "You won't. Let her assume it was an accident, and don't tell anyone else that the box and its contents are missing."

"What about Ruby?" I asked. "I'll have to tell her something."

He thought for a moment. "You tell her the truth. There was a small fire. I doubt she'll assume that Bert's stuff was burned up."

"But what if she asks me specifically about it? Then what?"

Amos sighed. "Then we'll deal with it, but I'd sure like to keep this as quiet as possible."

"You're hoping we can catch the thief before he disposes of everything."

"Actually, I was hoping that *I* could catch the thief before he disposes of everything, but I suppose there isn't any earthly way to keep you out of this." He flashed me a hopeful smile. "Is there?"

I returned his smile with one of my own. "Not in this lifetime, bucko. Not after the scumbag set my bookstore on fire and almost scared the life out of Miss Skiffins."

"I figured that. And don't call me bucko ever again."

"Okay. Now what's our first move?"

Amos started the car and pulled back out into the street. "First we get you settled in. Then, without much sleep, we go see Harvey. After that, you entertain your parents while I sniff around a little bit."

I started to protest.

"Don't get snarky," Amos interrupted. "I'll keep you updated on anything I find out."

"You bet you will," I said emphatically. "And you shouldn't say 'snarky'. It doesn't sound right coming from you."

"I'm trying to update my vocabulary. I have you to thank for it."

"Glad I could help," I said. "Now, out of curiosity, just where are you taking me? I'm certain we're not going to your place. You know I can't stay with you."

He nodded. "It wouldn't just cause a scandal; I don't have a spare bedroom. In fact, I don't even have a bedroom. I sleep on the couch."

"But you still live in your mom's old house. I thought there were two bedrooms."

"There were. But I let RoseAnn Flattery store

some of the things she inherited from her mother in one room, and Bubba Weber needed a place to keep extra jars of honey."

"It takes a whole room to collect a few jars of honey?"

Amos grinned. "If you're storing over a thousand jars, it does."

My mouth dropped open. "A thousand jars? My goodness! I know he sells a lot of honey, but surely you can't stockpile it too long without it going bad."

"He sells some; then he brings more jars. Besides, raw honey keeps almost forever, according to Bubba. Something about low moisture content. I wasn't really listening."

"Amos, you're a saint, and I appreciate your desire to help people, but do you really think you should have given up both of your bedrooms?"

He shrugged. "Maybe not, but I was spending most of my nights on the couch anyway. It made sense at the time."

I was pretty sure Amos wasn't happy living in the same house he'd shared with his mother and father. It had been a sad little house with peeling paint and a broken-down porch when his parents lived there. I'd visited a few times when we were young, but he hardly ever invited me over. Now we never mentioned it. Even though Amos had fixed the house up, we still never went there. It was as if it was a part of a past we weren't allowed to share. I didn't push it, although I felt that someday we would have to talk more about his childhood.

"So back to my original question. Where are we going?" I valued my privacy and wasn't interested in giving it up to stay with someone else, no matter how well intentioned they were.

Amos didn't answer me, but when he turned onto Oak Road, I knew the answer. "The Biddle house? Are you serious?"

The beautiful, cornflower blue Victorian structure that sat next to Lake Winter Break was my favorite house in the entire world. It was my dream home. Cecil and Marion Biddle had left it behind several years ago when they moved to Florida because of Cecil's arthritis. The icy Winter Break weather had been too much for him. They had rented out the house for a while, but thankfully, the woman living there was gone from Winter Break.

"But how—," I started to ask.

"Cecil called me yesterday to tell me that someone was going to be staying in the house for a week or so," Amos said. "He left me a set of keys and asked if I would unlock the house. I planned to tell you at dinner, but as you know, things got a little crazy and I forgot. I'm sorry."

"I don't understand," I said. "Someone else will be staying there, too? Who—" Then it hit me. "Wait a minute. Oh no. . . ."

Amos pulled up in front of the Biddle house.

"Now, Ivy. It's a big house, and they are your parents. You'll be fine. Besides, we'll get the bookstore fixed before you know it."

The sense of dread I'd felt since I found out my parents were coming to Winter Break grew little legs and started dancing the cha-cha in my intestines. "How in the world did my parents get hold of the Biddles?"

"I have no idea. Maybe they kept in touch. Your mom and dad have been to Winter Break more than once. If I remember right, they really connected with Marion and Cecil."

I'd forgotten about that. "But I don't see how they knew to reach them in Florida."

"Maybe you should ask Dewey. My guess is that he hooked them up. Your mom used to call him when Bitty broke her leg several years ago. He knew the Biddles had rented out the house before."

That was most likely the answer. Dewey probably thought he was doing me a favor. "I don't think this is a good idea, Amos. I'll be an easy target here. At least at home, I can get away if I need to."

"Ivy," Amos said forcefully, "your parents aren't your enemies, for goodness' sake! You should be thankful you have parents who love you." He glared at me in frustration. "Some of us would give anything for that."

Amos's chastisement hit home. My attitude *was* negative. It wasn't going to help me get along with my parents, and I was certain it wasn't pleasing to God. I sent up a silent prayer, asking the Lord to help me change before my folks arrived.

Amos carried my luggage inside the house. Everything looked just as it had when I was a child. The Biddles had left almost all their furniture and appliances behind, choosing to buy new things in Florida rather than try to transport all their belongings. The beautiful decor was perfect for the house. Comfortable, with a Victorian influence, the lovely maroon, gold, and cerulean colors were a theme carried into each room.

My favorite room was the huge dining room. One entire wall was made up of windows, with French doors that opened out to the patio. It offered a beautiful view of Lake Winter Break. Marion had hosted many dinner parties around the gorgeous mahogany dining room set that was positioned just in front of the windows. In the summer, the adults would eat inside with the doors open, and the kids would eat on the patio. I could almost smell Cecil's famous barbequed ribs as they crackled on the grill.

The thing I loved most in the room was a tapestry that hung on the wall, over the buffet. It was huge—at least seven feet long and six feet across. Marion had painted it herself. There was the lake, with children skating and snow falling. Cecil's flagpole was visible, with his little yellow flag waving in the wind. It was our sign that the water had frozen hard enough for skating. Once the yellow flag went up, children raced to the lake, where we spent hours and hours skating and drinking Marion's hot chocolate.

I could pick out each person in the painting. Amos and I skated together, holding hands. My best friend,

Emily Baumgartner, sat on a bench near the lake while accepting a cup of hot chocolate from Buddy Taylor. I'd forgotten about that. How touching that Marion had painted them together since they were now married. I'd had no idea that they had been anything more than friends. Had Marion seen something the rest of us hadn't? I decided to ask her about it someday.

I lightly touched the image of Aunt Bitty, sitting next to Emily, waving to me with one hand while holding a book with the other one. That was Aunt Bitty all right. Her great-niece and her books. Her two favorite things.

"That painting is very special, isn't it?"

I jumped involuntarily. I'd forgotten for a moment that Amos had followed me inside.

"Yes," I said softly. "It's very, very special. I'm still surprised that Marion left it here."

Amos set my bags down. "She said it belonged to Winter Break."

I was so entranced by the tapestry, I didn't respond. He seemed to understand and came up next to me, pulling me close to him. We stood there for quite a while, locked in an embrace, staring at Marion's labor of love.

When Amos finally spoke, his voice cracked with emotion. "The first time I ever saw you, you were only seven years old. You were standing next to the lake with your skates in your hands. Big white flakes of snow swirled around you, and the glow from the Biddles' backyard light made you look like an angel. You were the most beautiful thing I'd ever seen. You took my breath away. I was only nine, but I knew I would love you forever. I've never wanted anyone else since that moment."

"And I was thinking you were the handsomest boy I'd ever seen," I said softly. "Until that moment, I thought boys were nothing more than a necessary nuisance. What I felt that night was something brand new. Something wonderful."

He leaned over and brushed my lips with his. "I'd better go," he whispered. "I'll be back at nine."

I let him go and watched him walk out the front door. I'd been brokenhearted when I first came back to Winter Break. Losing Aunt Bitty was devastating. Funny how a little bit of time could change everything. I'd not only found a new life for myself in this small town, but I'd rediscovered love, as well. I knew beyond a shadow of a doubt that there was absolutely nothing in this world that could make me leave Winter Break. Not my parents and not the person who had tried to burn down my store.

I felt a kind of resolve inside that I'd never experienced before. Anyone who thought I could be run out of town was in for the fight of a lifetime.

I grabbed my bags, put Miss Skiffins's pet carrier under my arm, and went upstairs. There were four bedrooms at the top of the stairs, along with two bathrooms, but I climbed one more set of stairs until I reached the door to the attic. I hadn't seen this room for many years, but I was hopeful things hadn't changed. Sure enough, when I switched on the light, I found another bedroom. It used to belong to Marion and Cecil's daughter, Mary. We'd spent many rainy days playing in her bedroom when we were children. Mary was now a doctor in Wichita. We'd had lunch a few times when I was going to school, and she'd told me about her bid to have a room away from her three brothers. Cecil had designed this attic room for her. It had a sloping ceiling, with a large window next to a bed covered with a beautiful handmade quilt. The window looked out on the lake. Around the window and across the ceiling were small stars painted with silver fluorescent paint. Mary had asked her father if he could "bring the stars inside," and he had given them to her. I put my bags in the large armoire that sat against the wall, let Miss Skiffins out of her carrier, and then plopped down on the bed without changing my clothes. The little cat curled up next to me; I was so tired, I was asleep within minutes.

I dreamed I was frantically searching for something hidden beneath a dark velvet sky of twinkling stars.

Thankfully, I woke up at seven and had time to shower and change before Amos arrived. I'd found some instant coffee in the cupboard and made a cup, but there wasn't much else on the shelves or in the refrigerator. I would have liked to shop for my mother and father so they would have food available when they arrived, but Mother was so picky I knew it wouldn't do any good. It was better if she went to Dewey's herself and selected whatever she wanted.

After a quick cup of coffee, Amos and I got in the patrol car and drove out to Harvey's.

"Let me tell him about it," Amos said as we neared the house. "You keep quiet and look remorseful."

"That won't be difficult," I said morosely. "I feel really bad about what I did. Funny how something can sound so right in your head and turn out so wrong when you actually do it."

Amos sighed. "Here's a revolutionary idea. You could listen to the person who tried to warn you not to listen to that voice in your head."

"I wish it were that easy. I don't like to be told what to do. It's one of my greatest weaknesses."

Amos reached over and patted my shoulder. "And one of your greatest strengths is your ability to face the truth about yourself, Ivy. Some people never do that."

"Some people don't get as much practice as I do," I said wryly.

As he laughed, I thought about asking why he'd done such an about-face over my problem with Harvey. Originally, he'd declared that I would have to face the music alone. Now he was telling me to be quiet and let him handle it. I was beginning to learn that if I let him have enough rope, I might not have to hang for my trespasses. While I was debating whether I could ethically use this personality trait to my advantage, he stopped the car and got out. He had just opened my door when Harvey came strolling around the side of the house. He stopped as soon as he saw us and shot me a look that could have frozen even Hiram Ledbetter's Life-Preserving Liniment. I was obviously in deep trouble. Suddenly, Amos's offer to speak for me seemed extremely appealing.

"Hey, Harvey," Amos called out. "Can we talk to you for a minute?"

Harvey looked at us as if we were foxes who had come to inspect his henhouse. "What do you want, Deputy?" he called out.

"Ivy is here to apologize to you," Amos said. "She knows she shouldn't have gone into the orchard without your permission. I hope you'll be understanding about it."

Harvey sidled up close to us, his thin, sallow face locked in a perpetual scowl. "Understanding? You two don't seem to be able to mind your own business. You already desecrated my orchard once, and here you go again. I ought to file a complaint with your superiors."

Amos removed his hat and ran a hand through his hair. "Now, Harvey," he said in a soothing tone, "you know Ivy and I were only kids when we dug those holes. And nothing was desecrated. We didn't hurt the trees at all."

"Well, you aren't kids now, are you?" Harvey hissed. "So what's your excuse this time?"

"Harvey," I interjected, "this was all my fault. I found that map and wanted to see what was buried in the orchard. Amos planned to ask your permission before we stepped one foot on your property. I was the one who jumped the gun. Amos didn't know anything about it."

Harvey spit a stream of tobacco juice onto the ground. "That doesn't surprise me one little bit," he said, brown liquid dribbling down his stubbly chin. He reached up to wipe it off, but his dirt-encrusted hand made an even bigger mess. "You were always trouble, Ivy Towers. You were a mess when you were a kid, and you're a mess now."

"Now just a minute," Amos said, taking a step forward. "There's no call to talk to Ivy like that. Either you can accept her apology and be done with it, or we can certainly take this to the next level."

I had no idea what the next level meant, but Harvey took a step backward. After another spittle projectile, he locked his bloodshot eyes onto me. His expression was as sour as his attitude.

"I guess we'll let it go this time, but I'd better not

ever find you on my property again, do you understand?"
he said, pointing his finger at me.

"I promise, Harvey," I said in a contrite voice.
"Unless you invite me, I have no intention of coming
anywhere near your place."

"You don't have to worry about any invitations,
Ivy Towers," he replied in a low voice. "None will be
forthcoming."

"I saw you at Ruby's yesterday," I said. "You know
that we found a lunch box buried in your orchard?
One that belonged to Bert Bird?"

"Just goes to show you two weren't the only brats
fooling around on my property," he said harshly. "If
you're asking me if I want it back, the answer is no. You
let Ruby keep it."

Amos touched my back with his hand. "Okay,
Harvey. I hope we can let bygones be bygones. Is there
anything else you have to say about the matter?"

Another stream of brown liquid hit the dirt. A few
drops splattered against Amos's boot, but he acted as
though he didn't notice.

"No, there's nothing else to say, Deputy, except
good day to you."

"Thank you, Harvey," I said in my humblest tone.
"You'll have no more problems from me."

I could hear Harvey mumble something under his
breath, but Amos was steering me so quickly toward
the car, I didn't catch it. I was pretty sure he wasn't
complimenting me on my hairstyle or wardrobe.

Once we were in the car, Amos blew out his breath between clenched teeth. "That old so-and-so can be meaner than a rattlesnake on a diet. I can hardly believe he used to host jamborees here for the Scouts. Doesn't sound like something he'd do."

"People change. I guess when his wife left him, it made him bitter. We should feel sorry for Harvey. I'm sure he's a lonely, sad man."

"Acting that way certainly won't change anything."

"That's true, Amos. Maybe Harvey needs a friend."

Amos swung around and stared at me. "For crying out loud. Now you want me to be best pals with Harvey Bruenwalder?"

"Well, maybe not best pals, but it wouldn't hurt for you to reach out to him a little." Harvey was the kind of person it would be easy to walk away from, but I could hear Aunt Bitty's voice in my head. *"God doesn't give us credit for loving the people who are easy to love, Ivy,"* she'd say. *"It's loving the unlovely that really shows Christ's love."*

"You beat all, you know that?" Amos said, shaking his head. "You want to help Harvey, a man who wouldn't care if he never laid eyes on you again, but you don't trust your own parents, who love you to pieces. Sometimes I can't figure you out at all."

I smiled sweetly at him. "Good. That will keep a little mystery in our relationship."

Amos grunted. "I don't think that will be a problem. You certainly keep me on my toes."

I decided it was time to change the subject. "At least Harvey didn't insist we return Bert's box."

Amos shook his head. "I'm not sure whether it's because of his compassion for Ruby or because he just couldn't care less about it. I guarantee you that if you'd actually uncovered the Lost Gambler's Gold, he'd be putting a claim on it."

We drove the rest of the way in silence. I was turning the situation with the store over in my mind, trying to figure out who would want to set fire to Winter Break's only bookstore and what Bert's paltry trinkets had to do with it. I had no idea what Amos was thinking, but my guess was that he was still worrying over Odie and those missing cows. I was concerned, too, but the bookstore fire had taken top priority in my mind.

As we pulled up to the Biddle house, I was surprised to see Dr. Lucy Barber's SUV parked in the circular driveway. Lucy and I had started out on the wrong foot after Aunt Bitty died, but now we got along just fine. I counted her among my friends. In fact, I quietly carried on the work my great-aunt had started by helping with bills and medicines for some of the townspeople who couldn't afford what they needed. Lucy donated everything she could, and I made up the difference. I was going to have to start making some money with the bookstore soon, however. Bitty's inheritance was getting smaller and smaller.

The only real tension between us now came from the fact that Amos and Lucy had dated a little before

I came to town. Amos hadn't been serious about her, and she had always known that he was in love with someone else, but she still wasn't thrilled when I showed up after Bitty died. And I wasn't sure that there weren't still some leftover feelings of resentment on her part. It wasn't obvious, just an undercurrent I thought I felt sometimes. Of course, my imagination could be running away with me again.

"I wonder why Lucy is here," I said. "How did she know I would be staying at the Biddles'?"

"I told her," Amos said. "I know you feel okay, but you breathed in a lot of smoke last night. I want her to take a look at you."

"Amos," I grumbled as he parked the car, "why don't you just ask me if I need to see a doctor? I'm not a child!"

He plastered a big, goofy grin on his face. "You'd better smile and act like everything's okay. If Lucy sees us fighting, she may think I'm available again."

I reached over and slapped his arm. "If you keep trying to run my life, you *will* be back on the market." Since there was no way to make an escape, I climbed out of the car, determined to make the best of it.

Lucy saw us and jumped down from her vehicle. "Hey, you two! It's been awhile."

"It took a fire at the bookstore to bring you around," I said. "I'm not sure I can come up with an encore to that. Maybe you could just stop by to say hi once in a while without all the drama."

Lucy chuckled. "I think I can do that. Let's get you inside so I can see if you're going to live one more day." She was carrying a paper bag and handed it to me.

"What's this?" I asked.

"Just some things I thought you might need. Amos told me you'd be staying here for a while. I was pretty sure there weren't many supplies, since the house has been vacant for so long."

I peered into the sack and saw coffee, sugar, milk, bread, butter, eggs, and bacon. My stomach rumbled in appreciation. "This means you have to stay for breakfast."

"I don't have much time, Ivy," she said. "I have several people to see this morning. But I would love a cup of coffee. I was out pretty late last night at Cyrus Penwiddie's place. He's got a bad case of shingles, and it took me a long time to get him comfortable."

"Did you catch any of the excitement surrounding our mysterious fire?" I asked as we entered the house.

Lucy shook her head. "No. Cyrus's place is almost two miles outside of town. I never actually came into Winter Break. I was shocked when Amos told me about it."

I got busy fixing a fresh pot of coffee. I definitely needed another caffeine kick in the pants. And I was pretty sure Amos was as tired as I was. A glance at the clock in the kitchen told me my parents could swoop down on me at any minute.

With the coffeemaker chortling in the background, Lucy inspected my throat with her trusty tongue depressor. "Any hoarseness? Difficulty breathing? Coughing spells? Mental confusion?"

I answered, "Nuh-uh," to each question. It's hard to say anything more coherent with a large wooden stick holding your tongue down.

"Can I take that last question?" Amos asked.

"I don't think so," Lucy said. "I assume any woman who gets herself mixed up with you is suffering some kind of dementia."

"Oh, very nice," Amos said, shaking his head. "I can't believe the trials I am forced to endure for love."

His hangdog expression made Lucy and me laugh. My laughter almost ended tragically, however. Guffawing with a tongue depressor down your throat is a recipe for disaster. Lucy pulled it out. "Sorry," she said.

"Well, now I *am* coughing," I sputtered.

"You look fine. I don't see anything to be concerned about. If you have any symptoms, let me know, okay?"

"Symptoms of what?" a loud feminine voice interjected.

I turned around to see my mother and father standing in the doorway. "Mom! Dad!" I said, trying to redirect the attention somewhere else. My next step was to state the obvious. "You're here!"

My father's face erupted into a broad grin, and his arms opened wide. I flew into them. I hadn't realized until that moment how much I needed one of my father's bear hugs.

"Hello, punkin. I've missed you so much."

"I've missed you, too, Daddy," I mumbled from the folds of his coat.

"Nice to see you, Amos," my dad said with his arms still wrapped around me.

"Good to see you, too, sir. It's been a long time."

"Symptoms of what, Ivy?" My mother's forceful voice cut through my brief but joyous reunion with my father.

"Why, hello, Mother," I said, stepping back. "I'm happy to see you."

She reached over and gave me a quick, perfunctory hug. "Quit trying to avoid the subject, Ivy," she retorted. "What symptoms?"

"Are you okay, honey?" my father asked. His face showed his concern. My mother's expression was the same one I'd seen all my life. She was waiting for my next major foul-up. I rarely disappointed her.

"There was a small fire in the bookstore last night, Mother," I said. "Amos was afraid I'd breathed in some smoke." I pointed toward Lucy. "Mom and Dad, I'd like you to meet Lucy Barber. She's Winter Break's doctor."

My mother extended her hand to Lucy. "I'm relieved to know that Winter Break *has* a doctor. It's nice to know you, Dr. Barber. Do you live nearby?"

Shoot and bother. My mother had some kind of advanced radar that always seemed to zoom in on anything I didn't want her to know. I'd never seen anything like it.

"No, Mrs. Towers, I live in Hugoton, but I come here frequently."

Mom looked as if she'd bitten into something sour. "What happens if there's a real emergency? How long does it take you to get here?"

Lucy, to her credit, responded with a relaxed smile. "I can get here in a little over thirty minutes. And I have a trained nursing assistant who can take care of things until I arrive." She turned to me. "I planned to tell you that Sarah Johnson is now stocked with emergency supplies in case of an accident or a sudden medical emergency. We've been working together for a couple of weeks. I hope this will help folks in Winter Break feel a little safer."

"That's a great idea, Lucy. Between you and Sarah, I'm sure we're covered." I smiled at my mother, hoping to convince her that I would survive should I accidentally set myself on fire or explode from eating one of Ruby's Redbird Burgers. "Lucy's very committed to us. In fact, she drove to Winter Break late last night because someone called her."

"Unfortunately, it was a case that Sarah couldn't handle," Lucy explained helpfully.

I threw a quick, stern look her way. I was pretty sure she was only making things worse. "But you drove here right away, right? As soon as you received the phone call?"

"Of. . .of course, I was happy to come," she said cheerfully, getting the hint. "Anything I can do to help. . ."

"I know everyone in Winter Break appreciates you." My saccharine attempt to build up Winter Break's doctor was starting to make me feel a little nauseated.

Lucy smiled broadly at all of us. "And to that end,

I'd better skedaddle. Bubba Weber got stung by one of his bees and thinks the wound is infected. If I don't get there soon, he'll start trying to treat himself. The last time he did that, he almost lost his hand."

"Thanks again," I said gratefully. "And don't forget what I said about stopping by sometime just to visit."

"I definitely will do that, Ivy," she said, eyeing my mother. "Maybe sometime in the next week or two?" Her question was code for *Will your mother be gone by then*?

"That sounds about right," I said as innocently as I could.

"It was very nice to meet you, Mr. and Mrs. Towers," she said as she made her getaway. "I hope you enjoy your stay in Winter Break."

"Nice to meet you, too, Dr. Barber," my dad said. "Maybe we'll see you again before we leave."

A look of panic crossed Lucy's face. She nodded and then quickly executed her escape.

"She's very attractive," Mother said. "Is she Indian?"

"She's part Cherokee," Amos said. "On her mother's side. Would you two like to sit down while Ivy and I get us some coffee?"

"Thanks, Amos," my dad said jovially. "We've been driving for quite a while. I'm a little tired. A cup of coffee sounds perfect."

My parents sat at the breakfast bar while I poured coffee and Amos put away the groceries, leaving the sugar and milk out in case anyone wanted some. My dad took his coffee with two spoons of sugar and a dollop of milk. My mom was a no-nonsense coffee drinker. Black. And the thicker the better. I drank my coffee black but couldn't stand thick, bitter coffee. My mother called my coffee "hot, dirty water." I handed her a cup. She took a sip and shook her head. I ignored her.

"I'm going to have to get out of here, too," Amos said. "But why don't I take your bags upstairs before I go?"

"Why, thank you," my dad said with a grin. "My back isn't what it used to be. I'd be grateful for the help." He reached into his pocket and pulled out a single car key with a rental tag attached to it. "If you'll just put everything at the top of the stairs, I'll move it into whatever room Margie picks."

I wanted to ask why my father couldn't pick their room, but we all knew the answer, so I kept quiet.

"So how long has Dr. Barber been serving Winter Break?" my mother asked as soon as Amos left the room.

"A couple of years, I think," I said. I had a bad feeling that we were going someplace I didn't want to go.

"Hmmm," Mom said, tapping her nails against her coffee cup. "Amos certainly seems to know a lot about her."

Bingo. There it was. "Yes, Mother," I said with a smile plastered on my face. "And before you go there, they dated for a while before I came back to town. It was never serious. It's been over for a long time, and Lucy and I get along fine. So you can quit looking for something that isn't there."

My mother's raised eyebrow was the sign that I'd

overreacted again. According to my mother, I was always overreacting.

"You said there was a small fire at the bookstore?" my dad asked, deftly changing the subject.

"Yes. It looks like it started at a receptacle." That wasn't a lie. It did start at the receptacle. I wasn't going to offer any information about *how* it started unless I was asked specifically.

"That old bookstore is a fire hazard," Mother huffed. "It should have been torn down a long time ago."

I could feel the blood rush to my head. My mother was an expert at pushing my buttons. I'd made a promise to myself that I wouldn't respond to any of her cutting remarks as long as she was in Winter Break. With great effort, I pushed back the words I really wanted to say. "The people who live here love that bookstore, Mother. And I love it. No one's going to tear it down."

"It's been years since I've seen the bookstore, Ivy," my dad said. "I'm looking forward to it. Let's get unpacked and settled; then we'll drive over there. We'll also need to buy some groceries while we're out."

"I do want to check on the bookstore," I said, "but we may have to wait a couple of days for any kind of a tour. There will have to be some repairs, and I'm sure it doesn't smell very good right now."

"So where are you staying?" Mother asked. "Surely you're not still living in that tiny room above the store."

"No, Mother. Not right now. Not until things are cleaned up."

"So where *are* you staying, Ivy?" Dad asked.

"Well, for a few days, I guess I'm staying here with you. If that's okay."

My father's round, cherubic face lit up. "How wonderful! We'll be a family again—at least for a little while."

I knew what he meant, but I wasn't sure we'd been a real family in a long time. My mother seemed pleased by this turn of events, although I was afraid it might be because she realized I was now a captive audience. *Will you walk into my parlor?* said the spider to the fly.

"That's wonderful," she said, smiling for the first time since she'd arrived. "This will give us plenty of time to talk."

Of course, her upbeat mood didn't last long. Miss Skiffins picked that moment to rub up against her leg.

"Ooooh!" my mother yelped. "Where did this mangy thing come from?"

The startled cat ran around the other side of the breakfast bar, obviously frightened by my mother's screeching. I hurried over to pick her up. "Mother! This is Miss Skiffins, Aunt Bitty's cat." I held the trembling animal, trying to calm her. "She's my cat now. Please don't holler at her. She's had it rough. First she loses Bitty, then she wakes up in the middle of a fire, and now she's away from her home."

"Oh, for pity's sake," my mother said. "It's just a cat, Ivy. I remember how you used to assign human traits to animals. It isn't healthy."

"Now, Marjorie Christine," my father said in a stern voice. "We're only going to be here for a short while. You can be nice to this precious little kitty during our visit. Let's not have any more yelling at the poor thing."

My father rarely stood up to my mother, but whenever he said "Marjorie Christine," which was my mother's real name, she backed down without a fight. It was one of the reasons my dad was my hero. In my whole life, he was the only person who had ever managed to control my mother.

She didn't say anything, but I knew, at least for now, this battle was on hold.

"I think that's everything," Amos said as he strode into the room. He handed the car key back to my father and then leaned over and kissed my cheek. "I'll call you later."

I wanted to grab his arm and beg him not to leave, but I couldn't. I flashed him my bravest smile and watched him walk out the front door.

"So let's plan our day," my dad said with a sparkle in his eyes. "I particularly want to eat at that wonderful restaurant in town. What was it called?"

"Ruby's Redbird Café."

"Oh my goodness," my mother said disgustedly. "Are you telling me that place is still open? They might as well pile their plates with lard and hand people a shovel."

My mother is a beautiful woman. Copper hair, creamy skin, and large emerald-colored eyes. While my looks are rather untamed and pedestrian, hers are refined and elegant. I'd always wanted to look like my mother, but for the first time in my life, I actually saw myself in her. And I didn't like it. Was that what I sounded like when I complained about Ruby's food?

"Ruby Bird is a wonderful cook, Mother. She goes out of her way to make things she thinks people will enjoy. I'm sure you can find something to your liking if you try." I felt a surge of emotion that I couldn't understand at first. But then it became clear. This was my home, and Ruby Bird was part of my family. If someone from Winter Break criticized my mother or father, I would feel the same way. Defensive.

My mother sniffed her disapproval. "Well, hopefully Dewey Tater will have some decent things in his store. I'll try to prepare some healthy meals for all of us."

I didn't say anything, but I had made a quick, silent pact with myself. No more holier-than-thou attitude toward Ruby and her restaurant.

I glanced at my watch. "Why don't you guys freshen up and unpack? Then we'll head over to Ruby's for lunch. After that, we can check on the bookstore and go to Dewey's."

Not going to work in Miss Bitty's Bygone Bookstore felt strange. I'd grown used to it. I loved living among old books and new friends. I was happy with my life, and this change in my routine left me feeling unsettled.

While my parents chose one of the upstairs rooms and unpacked, I went out through the dining room and onto the large patio deck that Cecil had built onto the back of the house. It was hard to add a feature as modern as a deck to a Victorian house and retain its style, but Cecil Biddle had done a marvelous job. The white, weathered boards reached out toward steps that led past blooming flower beds to a dock that stretched almost twenty feet into the lake. I'd spent many hours sitting on that dock, wiggling my toes in the water while I thought about all the things young girls think about.

I sat down in one of the wooden deck chairs and breathed in the warming air, fragrant with the scent of honeysuckle and lilac bushes. I spent a few minutes thanking God for the day ahead and praying that He would help me to walk in love. *This is the day the Lord has made. I will rejoice and be glad in it.* I felt God's peace settle over me. Everything would be okay. *Love never fails.*

As I meditated on the unfailing goodness of God, I wondered what He had planned for my life. I knew He had a design, and that it was good, but I was the kind of person who always wanted to know what was coming. I was learning that God doesn't always lay things out ahead of time. Learning to trust Him was more important than knowing everything before it happened. "I trust You, Lord," I whispered. "Help me to walk in Your will and stay on the path You have laid out for me. Please help me to forgive the person who set fire to the bookstore, but help us to find out why whoever it was took Bert's things." Then another thought crossed my mind. "And, Lord, if he's alive, please bring Bert Bird home. Ruby needs to see her son again."

I felt a sense of peace come over me. That, coupled with the lack of sleep from the night before, caused me to doze off. Right before my mother woke me up, I thought I heard Aunt Bitty whisper, *"God does have a plan, Ivy. Someday soon, you will bring Bert Bird home."*

Since my mother wanted to go to the grocery store first, we decided to have lunch afterward then visit the bookstore. From across the street I could see Milton and his sons clearing out burned boards and working on a new door. I wanted to go over and help them, but I knew I'd just be in the way. I waved at them, and then I followed my parents into the Food-a-Rama. I'd found out that it *was* Dewey who'd suggested my parents stay at the Biddle house. I intended to thank him for his suggestion later, in private. It didn't take long, however, before I realized it wasn't necessary. Dewey was already suffering for his interference in my life. Although it wasn't any surprise to me, our trip to Laban's Food-a-Rama wasn't a great success.

"You don't have rice flour?" Mother asked when Dewey handed her a bag of regular white flour.

Dewey scratched his head and looked puzzled. "Sorry, Margie, but I only sell white and wheat. I didn't even know they made flour from rice."

"It's fine, Dewey," my dad said. "Flour is flour."

"Flour is not flour," my mother huffed. "I can't make *changfen* with white rice. And there's no sesame seed oil. Thank goodness you can buy rice in Winter Break. At least we can still have *congee* for breakfast."

"I said it's fine, Margie. Why don't you just cook

some of the good old American dishes you used to make? We'll have lots of time to eat Chinese food when we get back." My dad frowned at my mother, who immediately stomped off to look at something on one of the shelves in the back of the store.

Dewey didn't seem offended by my mother's less-than-gracious attitude. His face held its usual good-natured expression, and his smile was still in place. While my father explained to him that changfen is rice noodles and congee is a kind of Chinese porridge, I grabbed a basket and did a little shopping of my own. If I had to stay with my parents for a while, I wanted some food I liked in the house. I grabbed some microwave popcorn, one of my favorite things, and added some natural peanut butter along with a jar of Bubba Weber's honey. Then I sorted through the fresh fruits and vegetables brought in by Winter Break residents. Some lettuce, radishes, carrots, and a few not-quite-ripe peaches also found their way into my basket. I was looking over the extra-virgin olive oil when my mother's voice behind me made me jump.

"Ivy, why in the world are you buying groceries? I asked you want you wanted. I intended to get enough for all of us."

"I don't expect you to provide for me completely, Mother," I said in as calm a voice as I could muster. "I've been taking care of myself for quite some time."

"What do you mean by that?"

My mother's sharp retort so surprised me, at first

I couldn't think of anything to say. "I—I didn't mean anything by it," I finally sputtered. "I just meant that I can cook for myself. I don't expect you to buy my food and prepare my meals."

"Buy whatever you want. You can choose to eat with your parents or by yourself. It's your prerogative."

As she whirled around and headed down another aisle, I stood there and wondered why it seemed that almost everything I said made my mother mad. It hadn't always been that way. At one time, we were very close. We'd started having problems a couple of years before they left for China. Most of it had been my fault. I'd seen their plans as some kind of personal rejection. I regretted the sniping that went on between us back then, wishing we'd used the time we had together more constructively. Of course, we were together now and things were just as bad.

I grabbed a few more items before I checked out with Dewey. Mother and Dad were already in the car by the time I got out. Since Mom had purchased some perishable items, we ran the groceries home before we went to Ruby's for lunch. The café was already packed by the time we arrived, but Ruby hollered at a couple of farmers to sit at the counter and get out of their booth so that "Ivy Tower's parents can have a good sit-down meal." I thought it was a sweet gesture, but my mother looked embarrassed.

"Mickey and Margie Towers!" Ruby yelled at them after they slid into their side of the booth. "It's been nigh on forever since you been to town. Where you been keepin' yourselves?"

While my dad explained their mission in China, my mother eyed the big chalkboard mounted on the wall, which served as the only available menu at Ruby's. We were on the other side of the room, so it was difficult to make out her rather shaky handwriting. My mother took her glasses out of her purse, put them on, and glared at the Winter Break residents crowded next to the cash register to pay their bills, since they were blocking her field of vision.

"Margie, put those glasses away," my father said sternly. "Redbird Burgers all around, Ruby," he said with a grin. "Next to seeing my only child, your burgers are the best thing in Winter Break."

Ruby put her hands on her narrow hips and smiled with approval. "For you, Mickey, I'll make 'em extra special."

She looked over at me as if she wanted to say something else, but I glanced away, unwilling to meet her eyes. I didn't want her to bring up the lunch box now. Not in front of my parents. The less they knew, the better. Besides, I still hadn't figured out how to tell Ruby that the box and its contents had disappeared. My ruse worked. She sailed down the aisle on her way to make her famous one-pound hamburgers with all the fixin's. Except for ketchup. Ruby didn't allow anyone to put ketchup on her burgers. In fact, the mere mention of this particular condiment had led to more than one banishment from Ruby's establishment. As far as Ruby was concerned, ketchup was made for fries and meatloaf—and that was it. Period.

I'd successfully steered clear of Redbird Burgers for a month and a half. I felt as if I'd lost most of the five pounds they had added to my hips. I guessed since I'd lost the weight once, I could do it again.

"Mickey Towers," my mother hissed. "Why in the world would you order me one of those horrible hamburgers? I don't want it! And heaven knows you don't need it."

I wasn't surprised. My mother was always nagging my dad about his weight. He wasn't really fat, just rotund. With a beard and a red costume, he would make the perfect Santa Claus. His soft, silver hair, sparkling eyes, and rosy cheeks made him a perfect match for the jolly old elf.

My father turned to her with a twinkle in his eye. "Then why did you tell me that Ruby's Redbird Burger was the best thing you ever tasted?"

"I—I never said any such thing," she sputtered, looking at me. "Why would you say that?"

"Yes, you did, Margie," my dad said, smiling. "You said it the very last time we were in Winter Break."

"I—I—I couldn't have." My mother's face was as red as the checkered tablecloth on the table.

"Marjorie Christine," my father said in a low voice, "you not only said it, but hamburger grease was dribbling down your chin at the time. I remember thinking how cute you looked." He gazed at her fondly; then he shook his finger at her. "Now loosen up a little bit. Let's try to enjoy our time here." A large smile spread across his face. "I intend to have some fun with my daughter and eat myself silly. We don't get this kind of food in China."

I was certain my mother had blocked out everything she had once liked about Winter Break—including Redbird Burgers. She'd always felt that Bitty had wasted her life here, and she was determined that I wouldn't do the same thing.

"Ivy, I need to put some gas in the rental car. Where's the nearest gas station?"

"You'll have to get back to the highway, Dad. There's a station about ten miles from here. No one in Winter Break sells gas."

"Well, my goodness. What if someone runs out?" my mother asked. "You're just out of luck?"

"No. Several people keep extra gas stockpiled on their farms in case they need it. Some people, like Dr. Barber, carry around a can of gas in the back of their vehicles, although it sure doesn't seem safe to me."

Before my mother had the chance to respond, an unpleasant, nasal voice interrupted our conversation.

"Well, who do we have here?" Bertha Pennypacker sidled up to our booth. Her dyed jet-black hair was tightly knotted in a frizzy ponytail, making her face look almost oriental. Before I had a chance to say anything, Bertha stuck her large hand out toward my father. "I'm Bertha Pennypacker, a friend of Ivy's." Her mouth opened in an expression that was supposed to be a smile but looked more like the effects of gas pains. I was trying figure out just when we became friends while my father shook her hand and introduced himself and my mother. Bertha extended her hand to my mother, which meant that she had to reach across my face. I realized that she was desperately trying to show me the large diamond ring that sparkled on one of her fat fingers.

"Goodness, Bertha," I said helpfully, "what a beautiful ring. Is it new?"

"Why yes, Ivy," she simpered. "My husband, Delbert, gave it to me as a birthday present." She giggled girlishly. All of her chins wiggled like out-of-control Jell-O. "Along with a brand-new car and a fur coat."

I wanted to ask her what she was going to do with a fur coat in May, but I didn't want to encourage her to share any more of her time with me. "Why, that's wonderful. I'm glad Delbert is doing so well for himself." It was common knowledge that the Pennypacker boys kept the farm going while Delbert spent most of his time partaking of Hiram Ledbetter's Life-Preserving Liniment.

"My parents are visiting from China," I said, changing the subject before we were subjected to any further details of the Pennypackers' sudden good fortune. But Bertha quickly revealed that she had another reason for stopping by my table.

"Why, Ivy," she said with a smirk, "I heard someone

set fire to your little store and stole that box you dug up in Harvey's orchard. How odd. Why would anyone want that silly little box?"

I was flabbergasted. How did Bertha know about that? Then I remembered Amos's reprimand about mentioning the theft in public. The only place it had happened was in the bookstore, right after the fire. Who had spilled the beans to Bertha? "Where did you hear a story like that, Bertha?"

That weird smile again. "Now I can't tell you that. Let's just say that a little birdie told me. You're not the only one in Winter Break with secrets, you know." With that comment, she slinked away. Well, okay, she waddled away, but it was as good as slinking.

"What in the world is that woman talking about?" my mother said as soon as Bertha was out of earshot. "Who set fire to the bookstore? And why are you digging in someone's orchard?"

Since I had no choice, I told my parents the story about Bert Bird's box, leaving out as many details as possible. I tried to give them enough to explain Bertha's comments, but not enough to alarm them. I deftly left out the part about Harvey and his tirade. I had just finished when Bonnie brought our hamburgers. Thankfully, their attention turned from me and onto Ruby's Redbird Burgers. That was fine with me. I wasn't certain, but I could have sworn that I saw a tear in my father's eye. My mother just shook her head and clucked her tongue at the monstrosity in front of her.

Ruby's Redbird Burger was so big nothing else would fit on the plate. Bonnie's next trip produced a large basket lined with napkins to soak up the grease from Ruby's homemade, fresh-cut french fries.

We bowed our heads as my father prayed what could easily be the fastest prayer ever recorded. Before I had a chance to say amen, he had chomped down on his burger. Melting cheddar cheese dripped from between the buns and plopped down on his plate.

He mumbled something that sounded like "Mmm-mm, dis a bey burber eva maba," which I translated into "Mmmmm, this is the best burger ever made." My mother rolled her eyes again, but she did slice off a piece of her hamburger with her knife and delicately put it in her mouth. She didn't comment, but she started chiseling away at a very determined pace, and her eyes seemed to glaze over a bit.

When my dad reached a resting point, he wiped his mouth and looked at me with concern. "So you think someone purposely took that box and set the fire? Why would anyone care about an old box buried by a boy who moved away so long ago?"

Shoot and bother. Ruby's burger had just taken second place. I was obviously up to bat again. "That's the million-dollar question, Dad," I said. "It doesn't make any sense. And actually, there are two boxes. Bert's old lunchbox and another box I used to protect his stuff. Trust me, there wasn't anything there of value, except perhaps to Bert and his mother."

"You need to stay out of it, Ivy," my mother said. "This isn't your concern."

"It's my concern when someone tries to destroy my bookstore, Mother. Besides, they ruined Aunt Bitty's desk. That desk meant a lot to me."

"You really do love that old bookstore, don't you, sweetheart?" my dad said gently. "I didn't realize—"

"Oh, Mickey, don't encourage her. What kind of a life will she have in Winter Break, Kansas? My goodness, Ivy, someone as talented and intelligent as you shouldn't allow herself to get trapped in a small town on its way to nowhere." My mother hit the side of the table with her slender hand. "Why can't you see that?"

"And why can't you understand that I'm not you, Mother?" I said a little more harshly than I meant to. "I have to live the life I feel God gave me. It may not be what you're called to do, but I love it here. I feel at home, and I haven't felt that for a long, long time. Not since the last time I was in Winter Break."

My mother's face turned crimson. Without another word, she scooted out of the booth and headed for the door. I started to get up, but my father grabbed my arm and pulled me back.

"Let her go," he said. "She has some things to work out. You can't do them for her."

I sighed in frustration. "Why does everything I say set her off? Why is she so mad at me?"

"She isn't mad at you, you know; she's unhappy with herself."

I plopped back down into my side of the booth. "What are you talking about, Dad? I'm pretty sure I'm the person she thinks is throwing her life away. Why should she be upset with herself?"

My father smiled at me. "Because she's afraid she's the one who made the wrong choices, honey." He cast one longing glance at the rest of his burger, but unselfishly he ignored the temptation and grabbed my hand. "You know your mother and I have always felt called to be missionaries. We've had China in our hearts for a long, long time. But I wanted to wait until you were settled down, maybe married. In my mind, being your father has always been the most important job God ever gave me."

"Mother certainly didn't feel that way," I said, trying to keep the bitterness out of my voice. "I've always felt like I was in the way of her real goals."

"And that's just it. She has come to the realization that she may have failed you some. It's tearing her up."

I couldn't believe what I was hearing. "Is that the real reason you guys took this trip?"

He patted my hand before letting go of it. "Well, for me it was a chance to see you. For your mother, however, it was. . ."

"A chance to redeem herself," I said.

"Yes. I'm afraid that's the truth." My father shook his head slowly. "I think she's decided that if she stops you from 'throwing your life away in Winter Break,' she will prove to herself that she really is a good mother."

"But, Dad, I really am happy here. I believe with all my heart that this is where I'm supposed to be."

"I see that, Ivy, and I'm happy for you. The tough part will be making your mother believe it."

I wanted to say that I shouldn't have to do that. At twenty-one, I was an adult and responsible for my own life.

A vision of Aunt Bitty and me sitting on the Biddles' dock one summer floated into my mind. I had just aired my latest complaint about my parents. "Ivy," she'd said with a smile as she dipped her bare toes into the lake, "I never had children, but I know what it's like to love a child." She scooted closer and put her arm around me. "I'm pretty sure the hardest part of being a parent must be letting go. Frankly, just thinking about it scares me. When you're here with me, I know where you are. I know you're safe. But when you're away from me, I worry about things that could hurt you. One of these days, your parents will have to watch you start your own life, without being near enough to catch you if you fall. It will be incredibly difficult for them. I have no idea how people without God in their lives survive it. It takes great faith, Ivy. It will be hardest for your mother when that day comes."

Once again, my wise aunt had foreseen my future. For the first time in a long time, I admitted to myself that I'd never really doubted my mother's love for me. My abandonment issues weren't all her fault. Some of them came from my own unwillingness to see my mother's point of view.

"We'll get through this, Dad," I said. "Thanks for telling me the truth. Hopefully it will help me to understand Mom a little more."

My father smiled and attacked the drippy remains of his burger with gusto. I chomped on my own Redbird Burger until all that was left were some of the messy innards. And speaking of innards, I felt as if mine were going to burst. I encouraged my dad to go for a walk with me to burn off some calories before I exploded. We paid Bonnie and scooted out the front door. I was glad Ruby was too busy to notice. Even though the lunch box was no longer a secret from my parents, I still didn't want to tell Ruby that her missing son's property was also missing. Of course, Bertha and her big mouth might end up solving the problem for me, but that wasn't the way I wanted to handle it. Ruby had a right to know, and it was my job to tell her. I wondered briefly if this might be something I could foist off on Amos, but I pushed the thought out of my mind. Using him to get me out of the mess with Harvey was enough. I needed to take responsibility for this one.

I figured Mom would be sitting in the car, but it was empty. "Maybe we should look for her," I said.

"I think we should let her be, Ivy. Sometimes your mom needs time to herself to work things out." He grabbed my hand as we strolled down the street. "One of the things I love so much about your mother is that when she's wrong, she'll eventually face it and apologize. Trust me; she's harder on herself than she is on anyone else—even you."

I stopped walking and grabbed my father's arm. "Dad, Amos said the same thing about me. Am I. . . I mean, am I. . ."

My father laughed. "Are you like your mother?" He stopped in the middle of the street and put his hands on my shoulders. "Why do you think you and your mother fight so much, Ivy? It's because you're so similar."

"I don't think I'd ever leave my daughter behind so I could go to some other country, Dad. That doesn't sound like me at all."

My father smiled one of those wise-father smiles that meant I was about to find myself on the losing end of an argument. "But you would drop out of school and move to a town so small most people in Kansas have never even heard of it because you're convinced it's what God wants you to do?"

"But that's not the same. . . ."

"Maybe it's not exactly the same situation, but can't you see that both of you are passionate about what you believe? You and your mother are both looking for God's will in your lives." He sighed. "Maybe your mother and I moved too quickly. Maybe our timing was a little off, I don't know. But your mother's passion for souls and her willingness to give up everything for the people she believes she is called to help makes me respect her more than I can say." My dad's eyes were moist. "And I feel the same way about you. You've taken a big step of faith because you believe you've found the place you belong. You're making a brand-new life, teaching yourself how to run a bookstore, and reaching out for love. That takes courage, sweetheart. The kind of courage I see in your mother." His voice caught as he looked into my eyes. "I am so proud of both of you."

I wanted to argue, but I couldn't. My mother and I *were* alike. Passionate, committed, and above all, just plain stubborn.

My father let go of my shoulders, and we continued our walk down Main Street. In Winter Break, that means you must stop and say hello to half the town before you get more than two blocks from your starting point. While Dad extended warm greetings to residents who remembered him and introduced himself to those who didn't, I considered his admonition. By the time we turned around and headed back to the car, I'd concluded that my father was a much wiser man than I'd ever realized. Maybe it was time to let my mother off the hook. Perhaps we could bury the hatchet and start all over. I hoped so. Even more important, I decided to spend some time on my knees about the situation. Although I could see that change was needed, God was the only One who could actually clean up my heart.

We were rounding the corner on our way back to the car when Elmer Buskins stepped out of Buskins Funeral Home. His thick gray eyebrows arched in surprise when he saw us. "Why hello, Ivy," he said. "Isn't this your father?" The only way I'd ever been able to describe Elmer's odd voice was to say it sounded somewhat like a cross between Darth Vader and Tweety Pie. Elmer's attempts to present himself the way he thought a solemn and proper funeral director should were ruined by his high-pitched voice and pronounced speech impediment. "I'm so happy to see you again, Mr. Towers," he said. Of course it came out "I'm toe happy to tee you again, Mittah Towahs."

My dad didn't miss a beat. "I'm happy to see you, too, Mr. Buskins. How long *has* it been? Five or six years?"

"At least that," Elmer said, smiling. "Please, I'd love for you to come inside and see what a blessing your daughter has been to me."

My father shot me a questioning look, but I shook my head and followed Elmer inside the funeral home. Just a few months before, Buskins Funeral Home had been a tattered and used-up secondhand Rose. Now the floors shone and the carpets were thick and plush. The lobby held beautiful high-backed chairs covered in velvet. The old, rickety furniture was gone. Style and elegance were the watchword at Buskins'. Even Elmer's bald head seemed shiner.

Billy Mumfree, who used to clean the building on the weekends, was sitting at a highly polished table over in one part of the large outer room. A couple sat with him, looking at an oversized album filled with pictures. Billy, whose biggest goal in life used to be doing a wheelie on his ever-present skateboard, was dressed in a dark suit, his once-scraggly hair trimmed and neatly combed. I'd heard that Elmer had hired Billy as an assistant.

"Why, Elmer, the place is beautiful," my dad said in a low voice so as not to disturb the couple talking to Billy. "I'm impressed."

Elmer steered us down the hall to his office. When he opened the door, I couldn't believe it. The walls had been repapered, the carpet replaced, and new furniture filled the room. Elmer pointed at two handsome leather chairs positioned in front of his English-style, cherrywood desk.

"Everything you see is because of your daughter," Elmer said. He looked at me. "You haven't told him?"

I shook my head. It wasn't a big thing—not as big as Elmer made it out to be. I felt my cheeks start to tingle. I'm sure I was beginning to resemble an overcooked beet, but Elmer ignored my obvious discomfort.

"Your daughter discovered that an old desk lamp I'd been using for years was actually a valuable antique. I was able to sell it for a little over sixty thousand dollars." Elmer's voice broke, and his round, owl-like eyes moistened. "That money saved my business. Now, not only do the people in Winter Break come here, but people from other towns entrust their loved ones to me because Buskins Funeral Home is a place they can be proud of."

"Why, Ivy," my dad said, "I didn't know you knew anything about antiques."

"I didn't—I *don't*. We can thank Aunt Bitty for that." I explained about finding an old book in the store that had a picture of the lamp in Elmer's office. That book had given me my first clue that the lamp was valuable. It showcased lamps made by the Handel Company. Once I found the lamp, a quick Internet check told me that Elmer had a gold mine sitting under years of dust and grime. I smiled at Elmer. "I like to think that somehow Aunt Bitty arranged the whole thing so she could thank Elmer for all his kindness to her."

"Well, I don't know about that," my father said, "but if she did have anything to do with it, I'm sure she needed her kindhearted great-niece to carry out her plan."

The attention from my dad felt great, but I was ready to change the subject. With hair the color of a red stoplight, I had no hope of blushing attractively. Before I had the chance to turn our conversation in a different direction, Elmer did it for me.

"I hear you found an old box that belonged to Bert Bird."

I sighed. "My goodness, does the whole town know about this?"

Elmer chuckled. "You've been in Winter Break long enough to know that news travels faster than the speed of light."

"Yeah," I said dryly. "As fast as the speed of Bertha Pennypacker's mouth."

Elmer nodded. "You got that right."

"Elmer, did you know Bert Bird?" I asked.

"Yes, in fact, he used to help me sometimes. After his father died, I would pay him to sweep out the place. I couldn't give him much, but I hoped that whatever he managed to earn here would help out his family a little."

"Were you surprised when he left?" I asked.

Elmer frowned. "Well, no. Ruby told everyone he was going to stay with relatives from out of town. Things were really tough for her then. What surprised me was that he never came back."

"Other people tell me he was so frustrated with trying to keep the farm going that he stayed away because it was too much for him."

Elmer leaned forward as if there might be someone else in the room besides my dad and me. "Ivy," he said in a low voice, "I never believed that. After his father's death, Bert's number one concern was his mother." He shook his head slowly. "That boy was dedicated to her. Yes, it might have been hard on him for a while there, but I still don't understand why he's stayed away all these years. It just doesn't make sense."

"Then what do you think happened, Elmer?"

"I think he's dead," he said softly. "If that boy could have come home, he would have." He shrugged his small, rounded shoulders.

Amos's story about overhearing Morley Watson and Dewey talk about Bert flooded my mind. "Surely someone would have been notified if he'd passed away, Elmer."

Elmer sighed. "Depends on how he died. Maybe there was foul play. We just handled a funeral for a man who disappeared from Dodge City a couple of years ago. Someone found his body buried in a field about ten miles out of town. The farmer that dug him up didn't even know it was a skeleton at first. Thought he'd uncovered some old tree roots."

I felt the blood drain from my head and run straight down to my toes. I stood up in an attempt to force the blood back up to my brain where I seriously needed it now. "And a city girl might think they're tree roots, too," I mumbled. "Elmer, I think you'd better find a shovel and follow me out to the peach orchard. I'm pretty sure I know just where we'll find Bert Bird."

10

After speaking to Amos, I hung up the phone harder than I meant to. I was more than a little miffed. He'd wanted to know why I hadn't realized that the "roots" Bert's medal had been stuck on were actually human bones. I admit that my answer could have been more gracious. "I have no idea why I didn't immediately jump to the conclusion that someone had buried a young boy in a peach grove, Amos," I'd responded sarcastically. "I mean, that's what any normal person would have realized right off the bat, right?"

After advising me to calm down, Amos told me he'd meet me at the grove. As I ran toward the car, followed closely by my father and Elmer, I saw my mother sitting in the passenger seat. Shoot and bother; now I'd have to tell her about the body. Another nail in the "Why would anyone want to live in Winter Break?" coffin.

We all jumped into the car while my dad tried to explain to my mother just where we were going. I slumped down in the backseat next to Elmer, hoping it would make me a smaller target. It occurred to me that since I hadn't buried Bert in the peach orchard, I shouldn't be feeling guilty. Somehow, though, I knew my mother would see this as a result of my choosing to live in Winter Break. Surely there was some kind of connection.

My mother listened to my father's rushed account of my morbid discovery without saying anything. It was a bad sign. Whenever my mother grew silent, things were spiraling into the danger zone.

On the way to the grove, I tried to quit thinking about Mom's reaction to this strange turn of events. Instead, I attempted to connect the pieces of an increasingly odd puzzle into a clearer picture. Was the person who buried Bert in the peach orchard the same person who stole his belongings? Was it Ruby? Was she trying to cover her tracks? Try as I might, I just couldn't make sense out of it. Ruby didn't seem like someone who would kill her own son. She was truly touched when she saw Bert's box and the things inside. Was something else going on here? What was I missing?"

My dad stopped the car, forcing me to abandon my rather confused ponderings.

"You're going to have to tell me where to go from here, honey," he said.

I looked out the car window. We were at the edge of the peach orchard. We had already passed Harvey's house. I was considering whether we should go back and tell him what we were doing when Amos's patrol card pulled up next to us. Harvey was in the passenger seat, glaring at me.

Amos got out of the car and walked up to my window. "Harvey's fit to be tied, Ivy," he said with a sigh. "He says you probably dug up some old animal bones. There are a few of them buried around here.

Are you sure these bones are human?"

"About as certain as I can be, Amos. I haven't seen a lot of human remains, so I'm going on instinct here, but something tells me that no one's rib cage should be resting under Bert Bird's most prized possessions."

The tone of my voice made his mouth tighten. "All right, all right. You're going to have to lead the way, because none of us have seen this spot. With the map gone, I hope you can still find it."

"Odd how everything connected to Bert Bird keeps disappearing just like Bert did," I said. "Do you see a pattern here, Deputy Sheriff Man?"

He crossed his arms and glowered at me. "Yes, I do. And don't ever call me Deputy Sheriff Man again. Got it?"

I nodded and batted my eyelashes at him. "Just follow me, O Great Detective."

My dad started pulling away before Amos could tell me not to call him O Great Detective. "Where are we going, Ivy?" he asked.

I directed him around the edge of the grove. A dirt road encircled the entire orchard. When we were close to the place where I'd found the box, I told him to stop. Amos and Harvey pulled up behind us, and we all piled out of our respective cars. Amos grabbed a shovel out of his trunk. Elmer took the shovel he'd thrown into our trunk before we left, and he stood next to Amos.

My dad held out his hand for Elmer's shovel. "You

shouldn't get the nice suit dirty," he said to Elmer with a smile. "Why don't you let me do this?"

Reluctantly, the funeral director handed it to him. I was somewhat relieved. Elmer was a small man, not used to physical labor. It would have certainly taken longer if he'd insisted on digging.

"Okay, Ivy," Amos said. "Lead the way."

Even though I didn't have the map to guide me, I was pretty sure I could find the spot. I noticed a big tree I thought looked familiar. Then I remembered something. "The spot is marked with a barrel tapper," I said.

"What's a barrel tapper?" my father asked.

While Amos explained the intricacies of a barrel tapper, I glanced back at my mother. She followed silently behind the rest of us, her eyes focused on the ground, which was rough and uneven. I had no idea what she was thinking, but I was pretty sure I wasn't going to enjoy the aftereffects of today's adventure.

The tree I thought I'd recognized suddenly loomed up in front of us. "I. . .I'm sure this is the place," I said, staring at the ground in front of the tree. The dirt had been recently turned over, but the barrel tapper was nowhere to be seen. I got down on my knees, thinking it might have simply fallen over.

"Forget it, Ivy," Amos said. "Anything could have happened to it. If you're sure this is the place you found the box, that's all we need."

I stood up and looked around me, trying to remember what I'd seen the day before. "Yes, I'm certain," I said finally. "This is definitely the place."

Amos turned to the indignant property owner, who stood with his arms crossed and his foot tapping out an angry refrain. "Harvey, is there any other reason for the dirt to be turned over here?"

"Of course," Harvey said. "If you'd bother looking around a little bit, you'd notice all kinds of holes around here. I'm replacing my irrigation system."

Amos didn't respond, but his eyes narrowed. I wasn't worried. When the bones were uncovered, I would be exonerated. In fact, I would be a hero, finally closing a thirty-year-old case. I kept these positive thoughts foremost in my mind when Amos and my dad dug down a foot. I even held on to them at the three-foot level. At about four feet down, they disappeared.

"Ivy," my father said as Amos helped him out of the empty hole, "there doesn't seem to be anything here. Are you sure this is where you found the box?"

Was I sure? Could this be the wrong spot? I was asking myself these questions when I remembered something. I walked over to the tree and felt along the side. Sure enough, there on the side of the trunk were the marks I'd made when I was trying to clean my shovel.

"This is it," I said, looking into the faces of four people whose expressions were anything but reassuring. "Someone has moved the body."

"See what I told you, Sheriff?" Harvey said in an explosion of emotion. "I tried to tell you this woman is crazy—off her rocker! It's about time you listened to me and did something about her. I don't want her ever to set foot on my property again. She's a menace—a real nutcase."

"Harvey," I said, trying to stop the torrent of anger flowing from him, "there really was something here. I swear I didn't make it up. I—I don't know what to say."

Harvey took a step toward me, his face twisted with rage. I saw Amos move his way, but before either one of them reached me, someone else stepped between us.

"Now you listen to me, Mr. Bruenwalder," my mother said in a tone that caused all of us to stop in our tracks. "You're not going to talk to my daughter that way. If Ivy says there was something buried here, then there was something buried here. It has obviously been moved. May I suggest that your energy would be better spent trying to find out who did it? And may I also point out that this person, whoever he is, also came onto your property without your permission? I guarantee you he wasn't here trying to do the right thing—like my daughter is." My mother pulled herself up to her complete height of five feet three inches and declared loudly, "And one more thing, sir. Don't you ever call my daughter crazy again. I hope I am making myself abundantly clear." My mother's emerald eyes flashed with anger, and her body trembled.

Harvey took two steps back. He looked as though he wanted to say something, but after seeing the expression on my mother's face, he clamped his lips tightly shut. It was probably a defensive move. I guess there's nothing more dangerous than an angry mother.

"I'm going to post someone out here for a while, Harvey," Amos said. "I don't want anyone else fooling around until we get a handle on this thing."

Harvey started to sputter something, but Amos stopped him. "This isn't up for debate, so let it be. And one other question: Just where were *you* last night?"

Harvey clucked his tongue several times. "Sorry, Sheriff, but trying to place the blame on me won't work. I was in Hugoton last night. Headed there right after your little show at Ruby's. I went to help my sister get ready for her garage sale. Didn't get back until about thirty minutes before you came by this morning. You can't pin anything on me."

"I'm sure your sister will confirm this, Harvey?"

He flashed Amos a self-satisfied smile. "Yes, she will. And so will the members of her church who were there, too."

"I hope they will. Right now, I'm taking you home. I want you to stay in town for the next few days. Do you understand?"

Harvey nodded, but he didn't look happy about it. Amos ordered him to get into the patrol car. As soon as Harvey was out of earshot, he sighed and shook his head.

"I can't pull anyone from the department in on this right now," he said to us in a low voice. "Even though we all believe Ivy, I have no proof there was a body here."

"Then how will you watch the orchard?" my dad asked.

"There are a couple of guys in town who will help me unofficially," he said. "That's all I can do. I doubt we'll catch anyone who shouldn't be here. I think they already got what they wanted."

"Amos," my dad said, "if you need me, I'd be willing to take a shift."

"Dad! I don't want you out here. What if something happened to you?"

"Now, Ivy," he said with a smile, "nothing is going to happen to me, and this will give me something to do. You know I'm not the kind of person who can just sit around and do nothing." He put his arm around me. "Besides, someone is trying to mess with my little girl. You couldn't keep me from getting involved if you tried. So don't."

They say that a daughter compares every man to her father. I guess it must be true. As I stared into my dad's clear, sky blue eyes, set into a kind face, I saw something in him that I recognized in Amos. Not only were their smiles the same, but so was their unwavering support for me. Even though we hadn't found a body, Amos was proceeding as if he had no doubt in my story.

As I gave my father a big hug, I breathed in his trademark Old Spice. "Thanks, Daddy," I whispered. When I pulled away from him, I turned toward my mother. "And thanks, Mom," I said. "What you said meant a lot to me."

I don't know exactly what I was expecting, but if I thought my relationship with my mother had turned some kind of corner, I was mistaken. "I don't want you to think I've changed my mind about this place, Ivy," she said with determination. "I still think you need to get out of Winter Break. Not only is this place a dead end, but now it's become dangerous, as well."

"So you think I should just cut and run, Mother?" I said, not able to keep a note of exasperation out of my voice. "I should leave Ruby behind to wonder what happened to her son? And I should let the person who tried to burn the bookstore walk away? Let the place that Bitty loved just cease to exist?" I shook my head in frustration. "It's not going to happen, Mother." I took a deep breath and tried to pull on any reserve of courage I had inside me. "Besides, I have no intention of leaving behind the man I love with all my heart."

To say that I knocked the wind out of my mother's sails was an understatement. I'm sure she'd been wondering about my relationship with Amos, but there it was. I'd just tossed my inner feelings out for everyone to see. I hoped they weren't going to get trampled on and thrown back to me. I wanted to look at Amos, but I couldn't.

My mother's eyes narrowed, and her lips became a thin line. She spun around and headed for the car. My father grinned at me and grabbed Amos's hand. After shaking it vigorously, he followed my mother and slid into the driver's seat next to her. I could hear him saying something, his tone hushed but firm. After discreetly waiting a bit until there was a lull in the conversation,

Elmer flashed Amos and me a broad smile before getting in the car.

I turned to find Amos standing only a few inches away from me. He put his hands on my shoulders. "Did you mean what you said?" he asked, his voice husky.

"Well, I didn't say it because I thought that declaring your love next to someone's grave site was particularly romantic." I stared up into his eyes and felt a little tickle run all the way through me and settle somewhere inside my toes. In fact, I think I actually felt them curl up a little.

Amos shook his head. "For once in your life, couldn't you just answer a question yes or no? You always have to give the long version of—"

I put my fingers on his lips. "Yes," I said softly. "The answer is yes."

Amos moved his right hand up to my face and held my chin. Then he leaned over and kissed me lightly on the lips. When he drew back, his expression was serious. "Why don't you keep practicing that? I have another question to ask you when things settle down a little."

I was grateful there was time for practice. At that particular moment, I couldn't seem to remember any words at all. He kissed me on the nose, got in his patrol car, and drove off, with Harvey still staring daggers at me.

11

After leaving the orchard and dropping Elmer off, we drove to the bookstore. I'd noticed Milton and his sons working around the place earlier when we were at the grocery store, but I wasn't prepared for what I discovered once we walked past my newly installed front door. At least ten other people were inside the bookstore cleaning, hammering, painting, and fixing things up. Pastor Ephraim Taylor and his son, Buddy, were replacing burned wallboard. Bev Taylor, the pastor's wife, was cleaning soot and grime from the floor. Emily was down on her knees, scrubbing one of the blackened carpets that lay on the wooden floor. Someone else was helping her, but I couldn't tell who it was since her back was turned to me. My eyes filled with tears of gratitude to see these dear friends working so hard to help me in a time of crisis. In the corner, several men were on their knees, tearing out charred flooring.

One of them turned and waved at me. "Hello there, Miss Ivy," Isaac said with a big grin. "Can you believe how fast this is going? In two or three days, we should have everything back to normal."

"That's wonderful, Isaac." I motioned toward my parents. "Do you remember my mom and dad?"

"Oh yes." He stood up and wiped his dirty hands on a denim apron he wore over his clothes. He stuck his hand out toward my father, who shook it heartily.

"How are you, Isaac?" my father asked. "I'm so glad you stayed on to help Ivy. I know you and Bitty were very close friends. I'm sure her death was devastating to you."

Isaac paused for a moment before answering. "Yes, yes, it was," he said quietly, "but God sent Ivy to take her place. If He hadn't, I might feel that Bitty was really gone. As it is, part of her lives on, not only in the bookstore, but in my life. I'm very grateful for your daughter."

My dad put his hand on Isaac's shoulder. "I'm very grateful for you, Isaac. I hear you were instrumental in getting Ivy out of here before the fire spread."

Isaac shook his head. "As you can see, the fire wasn't that bad. She would have easily made it out without my help."

"But you were there for her. That means a lot to her mother and me. We know that someone is looking out for her in our absence. Thank you."

Isaac looked embarrassed, but I could tell my father's sincere appreciation for his intervention meant a lot to him. After a quick, shy smile, he turned around and went back to work. Isaac felt like a part of my family. But I guess that's the way it's supposed to be with Christians. We really are family. Unfortunately, while some people take the concept to heart, others, like Bertha Pennypacker, don't ever seem to understand it.

I stepped carefully over the holes in the floor caused by burned boards being ripped out and touched Pastor Taylor on the back.

"Ivy!" he said when he'd turned around. "How good to see you." He leaned over and hugged me. Spackling dust left a mark on my dark blue sweatshirt. "Oh, I'm so sorry," he said. "Look what I've done."

"Don't be silly," I said, smiling at him. "You could pour that whole pail of spackle on my head, and it wouldn't matter one bit. I don't know how to thank you for what you're doing."

"Helping someone you love is a joy. We're having a wonderful time."

"Pastor, I need to reimburse everyone for all these supplies. I hope you intend to give me the receipts."

"Ivy, Ivy, Ivy," he responded with a grin, "do you want us to lose our blessing? You know the Lord repays a lot better than you can. I think I'll take those blessings that are 'shaken together and running over' if you don't mind. I can't speak for anyone else here. You might get a bill or two, but I wouldn't count on it."

I couldn't think of anything to say. I truly believed Luke 6:38. I'd seen it work time and time again. Finally, I said, "I know we have some kind of insurance. I paid the bill not long after Bitty died. It's possible that it will cover some of this restoration. I'll check it out. In the meantime, will you please tell everyone that if they need reimbursement, all they have to do is let me know? Whether the insurance covers it or I do, I don't want anyone to feel stuck."

He nodded. "I'll be happy to, but I wouldn't be pulling out your checkbook anytime soon."

Fortunately, my parents picked that moment to find me, interrupting our conversation before I began to blubber with gratitude. "Pastor Taylor, do you remember my father, Mickey Towers, and my mother, Marjorie Towers?"

Pastor Taylor took off his gloves and shook hands with my parents. "Of course, I remember you both. It's been a long time. I understand you're ministering in China now? Bitty was so proud of both of you. She used to talk about you all the time." He paused for a moment. "Say, I wonder if you might talk about your ministry tonight at church. Just tell us what you're doing and how things are going over there. If this isn't enough notice, I'll completely understand. Maybe we can schedule it for another day." The hopeful look on his face made me smile. Pastor Taylor was so interested in missions, I almost wondered if he wasn't going to hop a plane to some overseas country one day.

My father gave one of his big Santa Claus laughs. And yes, it actually sounded like "*Ho, ho, ho.*" "Pastor," he said, "as you get to know us better, you'll discover we have no problem talking about our ministry. We'd be delighted to speak in the service tonight. You just point at us when you're ready, and we'll be more than happy to spend a few minutes sharing our adventures in China."

"Great!" When he slapped my dad on the back, a small plume of white dust rose from his glove.

"Ephraim Taylor!" a voice rang out. "Quit messing

up those people's clothes." His wife, Bev, came up and greeted my parents. Soon she and my mother were jabbering away like two jaybirds on a telephone line. My mother could be quite cordial to other people. It just didn't seem to extend to me.

My dad took off his jacket and was soon working away with Pastor Taylor. I decided to see if I could help Emily. She seemed focused on the rug, and when I patted her on the arm, she jumped. "Ivy!" she exclaimed. "I didn't realize you were here."

The girl working with her turned around. I was shocked to see a pale face with eyes outlined in dark eyeliner and lips smeared with dark red, almost black lipstick. Although she wore an apron over her clothes, she was dressed all in black. Her eyebrow was pierced. Seeing someone dressed in Goth regalia in Winter Break was a definite shock. I'm sure my face showed it.

"Ivy, this is Faith," Emily said. "She's my second cousin. Her mother and father passed away in an automobile accident last month. Faith has come here to live with us."

I was certain there was more to that story, but this wasn't the time to ask questions. "I'm happy to meet you, Faith," I said gently. "I'm so sorry for your loss. I can't thank you enough for helping out."

The girl glared at me. "She made me come here," was all she said.

"Well. . .well, still, I appreciate it."

"Whatever," the girl said, turning her back to me

and directing her concentration back to the job at hand.

"You keep at it; I'll be right back," Emily said as she stood up. She grabbed my hand and pulled me a few feet away from all the action. "I just have to tell you something," she said with a big grin on her face. "We just found out. I'm pregnant!"

I started to squeal, but Emily clamped her hand on my mouth. "Shhhh," she said. "Pervis might hear you."

I was more than a little confused. Pervis, Milton and Mavis's son, was a Baumgartner like Emily. I figured the Baumgartners shared everything.

"Pervis is dating May Pennypacker," she whispered. "If he hears you and tells May, she'll tell her mother and it will be all over town by nightfall. Buddy and I want a little time to tell people in our own way. I know you understand." She gently removed her hand from my mouth.

"Of course I understand," I whispered back. "I'm so excited for you!"

Emily's deep cocoa-colored eyes glowed. "You know, Ivy, I may have a large family—okay, an insanely large family—but when we were kids, you were more like a sister to me than any of my real sisters. I'm so glad you came back to Winter Break."

Simultaneously, our eyes filled with tears—which made us laugh. "What a pair," I said, attempting to choke back something that tried to combine a laugh and a sob. It reminded me of the story Emily had told me when we were young, about some man who supposedly coughed, hiccupped, sneezed, and laughed all at the same time. With eyes as big as saucers, Emily had said the man dropped dead. Until I was almost sixteen, whenever I got a cold, I worried that I might be attacked by that deadly combination. I reminded my friend about her odd story, and we launched into a spasm of laughter. I glanced behind us to see several people watching us with concern. Unfortunately, it just made everything funnier. I was certain my Winter Break friends had decided that the fire had dislodged the last loose screw holding my sanity together. After a couple of minutes, we were able to find a measure of control. With a promise to call me later, Emily went back to work.

I was going through a few books on the shelves, sniffing them to see if they smelled like smoke, when someone called my name. It was Isaac.

"I heard you mention something about insurance to Pastor Taylor," he said. "Miss Bitty had insurance on the bookstore through the Farm and Field Insurance Company in Dodge City. Some man named Shackleford was the agent. Unfortunately, the deductible was so high, I'm sure it won't help you." He sighed. "Bitty didn't want to spend money on insurance. She got the cheapest policy she could."

I patted his shoulder. "I'm not really surprised. I think she knew that if something happened, she was covered. Either by angels or the people of this town." I struggled to contain the overwhelming gratitude that threatened to surface and turn me into a sobbing mass of jelly. "Right now, it's hard for me to see much of a difference between the two."

Isaac nodded. "I've felt that way myself many times."

After he walked away, I went back to checking the books. To my relief, they seemed fine. Mavis must have been right. The smoke had drifted toward the front door and the windows. There's something to be said for drafty old bookstores that aren't completely airtight.

At one point, Milton and his sons took me over to the new door to show me their workmanship. They had installed the door along with a beautiful carved frame that surrounded the outside entrance. It was perfect. My concerns about losing the original door evaporated.

"It looks like wood, don't it?" Milton said with a lopsided grin.

I agreed that it certainly did.

"Nope," he said with an air of pride. "Solid steel. Ain't nobody gonna be able to knock this thing down." He reached into his pocket and pulled out a set of keys. "These are yours. This one is to the doorknob, and this one is for the deadbolt."

I thanked him and took the keys. I was about to ask him how much the door cost when I noticed Pervis picking up supplies from the front porch. I excused myself and ran down the steps in an attempt to stop him before he got into his truck.

"Pervis," I called out. "Can you wait just a minute?"

He paused at the back of the truck and stared at

me. Pervis was a good-looking kid. Tall and lanky, he'd inherited his mother's height and coloring, but thankfully for him, his other features were more directly connected to his father.

"Pervis," I said, "first of all I want to thank you for everything you're doing for me. There's no way I could ever repay your kindness."

A slow smile spread across his freckled face. "It's no problem." His voice was surprisingly deep. "I'm happy to do it."

"I hope you won't be offended by my next question." Even before I asked it, Pervis cast his eyes toward the ground, looking distinctly uncomfortable.

"The night of the fire, I noticed that two boxes that were sitting on my desk were missing. I only mentioned it to Amos, but somehow the story got out. I wonder if you know how that happened."

At my words, his face fell. "I'm real sorry, Ivy," he said. "I overheard what you said and mentioned it in passing to May Pennypacker. I think she told her mama. I wouldn't have said a word if I'd realized what would happen. May and I had a long talk about it. I told her that spreading tales was a sin and that I didn't cotton to it." The look of remorse on his face was real. "May feels real bad about it, too. It's caused some real trouble between her and her mama."

"I'm sorry to hear that, Pervis. I hope you learned a lesson here, though. Spreading stories can cause a lot of problems. I really didn't want anyone to know that the boxes were missing."

With that, Pervis looked so upset, I had to put him out of his misery. "Let's not worry about it anymore, okay? What happened, happened. But I would appreciate it if you would keep anything else you hear about me to yourself. Do you think you can do that?"

Shamefaced, he hung his head. "Yes. You have my word."

I reached over and touched his arm. "Thanks, Pervis. Now let's forget about it, okay?"

"Okay," he mumbled. He got into his truck, and I started back up the stairs. I felt sorry for him, and I really didn't blame him for what Bertha did with the information he'd inadvertently given her. That was on her. Of course, now that she'd spread the story all over town, it was going to make finding out who took the box a lot more difficult.

Before I got to the door, I noticed Alma Pettibone coming toward me, carrying a large plastic box. I raised my hand in greeting. "Hi, Alma. What have you got there?"

She almost flew up the stairs. "I just thought with everyone working so hard, maybe they'd like some cookies and lemonade. If you'll take these inside, I'll go back and get my thermos and some cups."

"Alma, that's such a nice thing to do. Thank you." It was then that I noticed that Alma's habitual topknot was gone. In its place was a lovely, soft hairstyle that framed her face with a silver glow. And she was wearing makeup. Not much, just enough to bring out her eyes. Funny that I'd never noticed she had such beautiful eyes. My question as to why Alma had changed her looks was answered only seconds after I held my hands out for the box. She hesitated for a moment after handing me the cookies. The container was heavier than I'd expected. There had to be seven or eight dozen cookies packed inside.

"I wonder. . . ," she said lightly, a blush spreading from her neck into her checks, "if Isaac is inside. I mean, is he one of the men working. . . I mean, do you know where he might. . . I mean. . ."

I could tell that if I didn't stop her, we would be standing on the steps all afternoon, waiting through hundreds of "I means."

"Alma," I said as kindly as I could, "Isaac is inside working. I know he'll really appreciate the cookies and lemonade. Why don't you go get your thermos and together we'll set this up in the store. Maybe you can stay and serve everyone." By everyone, I meant Isaac.

"That would be. . . I mean. . .that would be wonderful, Ivy," she said. As she scurried down the steps, I was left with the distinct impression that Dewey wasn't going to have to worry about unwanted attention from Alma Pettibone anymore. Isaac and Alma. Interesting. Under normal circumstances, it was a relationship I wouldn't place any bets on. But when the bell over the church rang three times, I realized that Alma Pettibone was missing one of her favorite soap operas,

The Gallant and the Gorgeous. Before today, I wouldn't have believed she'd miss that sordid tale for anything. "Wow," I whispered to myself, "there's a lot more than flowers in bloom in Winter Break, Kansas."

As I started back up the steps, I noticed something sticking out from underneath a pile of lumber. I put the cookie box down, walked to the bottom of the steps, and moved the boards aside. I reached down and pulled out a gas can. Somebody had piled building supplies on top of it, probably not realizing that it might belong to the person who started the fire. Although it appeared to be just like every other gas can I'd seen in Winter Break, I looked it over carefully for any signs of ownership. When I turned it over, there, written in marker on the bottom of the can, were the initials LB.

Lucy Barber.

12

Amos was late getting to church that night. I deposited my parents in the sanctuary and waited in the lobby as long as I could, but I finally gave up and went inside. I'd have to wait until after the service to tell him what I'd found. I couldn't help but wonder how he would react. Would he defend Lucy? Would he believe she'd started the fire? I certainly had my doubts. The only reason I could come up with for her wanting to burn down the bookstore would be to get me out of town. I had to admit to myself that I'd been wondering if she still had feelings for Amos, but I just couldn't see her doing something like this. Since coming to Winter Break, I'd discovered that she was a compassionate doctor who cared deeply about people. So what were the alternatives? Could the initials belong to someone else? Was it possible the gas can had been stolen and left by the steps to throw suspicion on Lucy? I had no idea what the truth was, but the one thing I was sure of was that the can was placed there for a reason. It hadn't been there before the fire; I would have noticed it. The gas can was one more piece of a puzzle that didn't seem to fit together into any final image that made sense.

I was turning all these things over in my mind when Pastor Taylor stepped up to the podium, and Amos slid into the pew next to me. He squeezed my arm and focused his attention on what the pastor was saying. I tried to listen, but my mind kept wandering. I caught Amos looking at me a couple of times. He could tell I was restless. I fumbled around in my purse until I found a scrap of paper. I scribbled, "I need to talk to you after church," on it then passed it to him when my mother was looking the other way. Here I was, twenty-one years old and worried that my mother might catch me passing a note in church. Amos took the slip of paper, read it, and then slid it into his pocket after nodding his agreement.

I forced myself to put my concerns about Lucy Barber on hold and pay attention to the sermon. Pastor Taylor was reading the story of the prodigal son in the fifteenth chapter of Luke. When he got to the part about the father welcoming his son home, I couldn't help but look across the room at Ruby. Was she thinking about her missing son? Where was Bert Bird? Was he really dead? And if so, who had killed him? I still couldn't believe it was Ruby, no matter what Dewey and Morley Watson might have said years ago. And whose bones had I found in the orchard? Harvey's claim that they were animal bones popped into my head. But time spent in biology classes told me they were human. Besides, why would someone go to all the trouble of moving old animal bones? That really didn't make any sense. My mind was churning over so many questions, I was giving myself a headache. Then I heard Aunt Bitty's voice whispering in my ear, *"Real faith means letting go, Ivy. If you ask God for something, you must believe He's working on the answer. If you're still chewing on it, that problem's still sitting on your plate.*" She was right, of course. I had a tendency to try to work everything out myself. I needed Him to show me the truth. A verse in Matthew popped into my mind. "There is nothing concealed that will not be disclosed, or hidden that will not be made known." I whispered a quiet prayer, asking God to reveal what was hidden and to help Ruby find peace. I also asked Him to bring Bert home if he was still alive. I suddenly realized that I was still staring at Ruby. But now she was looking right back at me, and the look on her face startled me. Was it anger that twisted her features? She turned her head away, but the expression on her face haunted me throughout the rest of the service.

About fifteen minutes before the time we normally dismissed on Wednesday nights, Pastor Taylor called my parents up front. As they talked about China, I heard something in my mother's voice I'd rarely heard before. Passion. My mother was passionate about China—about the people who lived there.

My dad began telling a story about a tour guide who was hired to show them around Hong Kong. While they were inside one of the many temples in and around the city, the small woman who was their guide pulled my father over to the side and said, "I understand you are a Christian minister?"

My father, a little concerned that she was going to object to his presence inside one of their holy sites, hesitantly admitted that he was.

"Oh, sir," the woman said with tears in her eyes, "I have been praying for twenty years for God to send someone to tell me about Jesus. Will you please tell me the story of the Savior?"

As my father shared that the woman was marvelously converted and now serves with them in China, I noticed that my mother was crying. How many times had she heard that story? Yet it still touched her. I began to understand that my mother only wanted me to feel the kind of fervor she did. She wasn't trying to ruin my life; she was trying to help me find it. I reached over and took Amos's hand. It was going to be my job to make her see that although my calling wasn't the same as hers, it was just as real and just as strong.

When Pastor Taylor closed the service, many of the parishioners rushed toward my parents. I could see I wasn't the only person touched by their story. With the welcome distraction, I grabbed Amos's arm and pulled him out of the sanctuary. The door to the library was unlocked, so we slipped inside. Although the main lights were off, a small lamp that sat on a table near two stuffed chairs gave out enough illumination for us to see.

I immediately launched into the story about finding the gas can with Lucy's initials. When I finished, Amos frowned.

"Ivy, I don't believe for one minute that Lucy set that fire. She just isn't that kind of person."

"I have to agree with you, Amos. For a while I wondered if Lucy was still madly in love with you. Maybe she tried to burn down the bookstore so I would leave town and she'd have you all to herself."

Amos shook his head. "First of all, Lucy Barber is not madly in love with me. I think I'd know. And second, how do you explain the theft of the boxes? Why would Lucy want them?"

I sighed. "She wouldn't. That's what's so confusing. Everything looks suspicious; the theft of the letter and the boxes, the fire—but nothing seems to connect." I grinned at him. "And as far Lucy goes, if she were crazy about you, you'd never know it. Men are absolutely clueless about love."

Amos grabbed me and pulled me close to him. "You're wrong there, you know. I know you're wildly, madly, and completely in love with me."

"You have quite an ego there, don't you, champ?"

"No," he said softly. "And don't call me champ."

My retort was curtailed by his kiss. Finally, I pushed him away. "Making out in the church library. You have no shame, do you?"

"No," he answered simply. "Come back here."

"Amos, stop it! We have to talk. I don't know when I'll get another chance. My parents follow me everywhere I go."

"Okay, okay," he said, plopping down in one of the chairs near the lamp. "But you owe me lots of lip time when they leave."

"Just keep a running total of my debt, will you?" His grumpy expression made me laugh.

I sat down in the chair on the other side of the table. "Why don't you ask Lucy about the gas can, Amos? Show it to her. Maybe she can shed some light on it. I'd like to know if it was stolen, and if so, when."

"I guess I can do that," he said, "but I'll do it in a way that won't make it seem like I'm accusing her of anything."

"Fine. I have it in my trunk. I'll give it to you when we leave."

"Is there anything else?"

"Yes." In the glow of the lamp, he looked so handsome I was having a hard time concentrating. I forced myself to gather my thoughts. "I've been thinking. The bones I saw could have belonged to Bert Bird. I mean, as far as we know, he's the only person who is missing from Winter Break. But the problem is, just how did Bert manage to die and then bury his treasure box on top of himself? It doesn't make sense."

Amos folded his arms across his chest and looked at the floor as he thought about what I'd said. I could almost hear gears turning in his head. Finally, he looked up. "You know, that *doesn't* make any sense. Unless he was killed while he was burying the box. Someone found him, killed him, and then buried him and the box."

"Okay, that's possible. But there's something else here I can't figure out."

"What?"

"Why did Bert want to bury his most treasured possessions in the first place? Why not just take them with him? Why draw a map so he could find them again? And how in the world did the map get inside Bitty's jewelry box? And the big question, why would anyone want to kill Bert Bird? What possible threat could he have been to anyone?" I turned to stare at Amos. He looked as puzzled as I felt.

"Those are good questions. I'm afraid I don't have answers for them," Amos said.

"One other thing I've been thinking about. I know Harvey said he wasn't in town during the time someone dug up the bones and moved them, but he could have done it. I mean, it is his property. He seems to be the most likely suspect."

"Why would he do that?" Amos asked. "Unless he put them there in the first place."

"Well, maybe he did."

Amos laughed. "So you think Harvey caught Bert digging in the orchard, got mad, whacked him, and threw in his lunch box for good measure? I think that's a little harsh even for Harvey. And besides, if he was that upset about Bert trespassing on his property, you and I should have been six feet under a long time ago."

"Okay. Point taken. Obviously someone else moved the bones." I reached over and grabbed his hand. "Look, this may be a waste of time, but I'd like to find out who else left town around the same time Bert did. He was just a boy. He probably wasn't traveling alone. Maybe he left with someone else—someone who dropped him off with these elusive relatives Ruby keeps mentioning."

"But what if Ruby's relatives came here to get him?"

"I think someone would have seen them, Amos. Winter Break is a pretty small town. I'm not saying it isn't possible, but so far, no one has mentioned anything like that."

"I don't know. That was a long time ago. I doubt we can find much."

"I know," I said. "But let's try. I'm going to talk to Dewey. He's been here forever, and people open up to him. Maybe he'll have some helpful information. And I'm also going to pay Bonnie a visit. If she was Bert's girlfriend, she might be able to shed some light on what happened when he left."

"You'd better do it when Ruby's not around. I don't think she'd appreciate your questioning her only employee." He shook his head. "You know, Ruby's the person we should be asking. She's the only one who really knows the truth."

"No," I said emphatically. "It's obvious she's not going to tell us anything. I think we need to keep her in the dark until we figure out what's going on. All we have right now are several strange occurrences that aren't leading us to anything solid. I don't want to stir her up with a bunch of meaningless suspicions."

"There's still the possibility she might be involved, Ivy. She's definitely keeping some kind of secret. I hope it doesn't turn out to be the worst-case scenario here, but you need to prepare yourself."

"Maybe. But do you really believe that Ruby set my bookstore on fire and moved Bert's body? I just don't see it."

Amos stood up, stretched, and yawned. "Right now I'm not thinking about much of anything except getting some sleep. I'm heading home, Ivy. It's been a long day."

"I forgot to ask you, how are things going with Odie? I saw him in the sanctuary. He didn't look too happy."

Amos ran his hand through his hair and sighed. "No, he's not happy at all. But the truth is, there isn't enough evidence to charge him with anything. And there isn't enough proof to let him off the hook, either. All I've managed to do is to make him feel defensive. It's not a good place for two Christian brothers to find themselves in. I don't know what to do."

I grabbed his arm and pulled myself up, leaning into his strong shoulder. "The thirteenth chapter of First Corinthians tell us that 'love always hopes, always perseveres.' I guess all you can do is persevere in believing the best about Odie."

Amos stroked my hair. "I wish I could do that," he said softly. "But as a law enforcement officer, my first reaction is usually suspicion."

"Maybe Odie senses that, Amos."

He kissed the top of my head. "You're probably right. Maybe I should sit down with him and talk to him like a brother. He needs to understand that just because I have to do my job, it doesn't mean I don't believe in his innocence."

"Do you believe he's innocent?"

Amos sighed so deeply, I felt my hair move. "You know, Ivy, I really do. I train myself not to make judgments on guilt or innocence. But I truly don't believe that Odie Rimrucker would steal cattle. I just don't."

I looked up and kissed him lightly on the lips. "Then tell him that."

"I will." After one more long, lingering kiss, he left the library. I wanted a few minutes to sort out my thoughts, and I knew I wouldn't get the chance for a while with my parents around. I'd just sat back down when I heard a noise behind one of the bookshelves. Wondering if there were mice in the library, I got up to check it out. Instead of a mouse, I found someone sitting on the floor in the corner. Hidden in the shadows, the lurker wasn't immediately identifiable, but a closer look revealed Faith, Emily's young Goth cousin.

"Faith, what are you doing here?"

"I wasn't trying to listen to you, if that's what you think," she said in a surly tone.

"I didn't say you were. I just wondered why you were in here instead of in the sanctuary."

She jumped to her feet and stepped into the light where I could see her. The black streaks under her eyes revealed that she'd been crying. "I don't like churches, and I don't believe in God."

162 Bye Bye Bertie

"And why is that?"

Her upper lip curled in a sneer. "I suppose if you believe in a God that would kill your parents, that's up to you. I sure don't." She pushed past me and headed toward the door.

"I don't believe in a God who would do that," I said toward her fleeing back. "I believe in a God who gives life, not death."

She whirled around and glared at me. "My cousin Emily says the same thing. So how do you explain what happened to my parents?"

I smiled at her in the dim light. "I don't. I didn't know your parents and wouldn't even begin to hazard a reason for their tragedy. But I will tell you that God doesn't go around killing people. We don't live in a perfect world, Faith. There's evil, pain, and tragedy. But God's not the author of it."

Her face crumbled with grief. "Then why didn't He save them?"

I walked up to her and put my hand on her arm. "I can't answer that either."

She pulled away from me and took two steps back. "You sure don't know much, do you, lady?"

"Maybe not," I said gently, "but I know that God is good, and I know He loves you very much. If you give Him a chance, someday He'll answer your questions. For now, though, I think you need to let Him help you through this."

She shook her head. "No thanks. I'm doing just fine without Him."

She turned and started for the door but then stopped with her hand on the doorknob and looked back at me. "This kid, Bert. The one you were talking about?"

Feeling that this wasn't the time to chide the girl for eavesdropping, I just nodded.

"He planned to come back."

"What do you mean?"

The light from the lamp illuminated her face—and the sadness I saw etched there. "He wouldn't have left things behind that meant so much to him. He would have taken them with him unless he planned to come back to them someday. It was like a promise, you know? A vow to return."

I started to ask her how she knew this but realized it wasn't necessary. I could see it in her eyes. She'd left something of her own behind, hoping that someday she'd go home. But in Faith's case, there didn't seem to be anyone to go home to. Without another word, she opened the door and left the library.

I pondered her words while I rounded up my parents and said good-bye to Pastor Taylor and his wife. Emily came up and hugged me, promising to get together with me later in the week. I noticed Faith standing behind her, but she wouldn't look at me or acknowledge my presence.

When we got to the parking lot, I saw that Amos's patrol car was gone. He'd left without getting the gas can. I made a mental note to remind myself to give it to him the next time I saw him. I also wanted to tell him what Faith had said about Bert. It made a lot of sense, but it also raised a lot of new questions. I chewed on everything while driving back to the Biddle house. My father was talking most of the way home, but I was so distracted I caught only part of what he said.

When we unlocked the front door and stepped inside, I heard my dad say, "Well, what do you suppose this is?"

He leaned down and picked up an envelope that had been slipped under the door. He handed it to me, since my name was scrawled on the front. I opened it while my parents stared at me. Inside, on a piece of paper, someone had written, "Don't look for Bert Bird unless you want to see someone get hurt."

13

After being grilled by my parents into the wee hours of the morning, I found it hard to roll out of bed with only a few hours' sleep. I'd called Amos after we found the letter, and he'd promised to come over in the morning to discuss it. I hurried around and tried to make myself look presentable. The circles under my eyes were still there after I touched them up with concealer, but at least they were less obvious.

I listened at the top of the stairs, hoping my parents had changed years of routine and slept late, but my hopes were dashed when I heard their voices in the kitchen. As I came down the stairs, my father was just going out the front door.

"Good morning, sunshine!" he called out. "I'm taking the rental car into Hugoton for some gas. We're sucking fumes. Is there anything you need from the big city?"

I laughed. "Hugoton really isn't very big. You might be disappointed."

He grinned. "If you could see some of the villages we've been to in China, I bet you'd think Hugoton was a progressive metropolis."

I shook my head at him, and he reached over and hugged me before going out the door. My mother sat at the kitchen counter with a look that told me our conversation from the night before wasn't finished.

"Before you say anything, Mother, Amos is supposed to be here any minute. Let's let him take a look at the letter before we jump to any further conclusions."

"Ivy Samantha Towers," she said, irritation spewing through each syllable of my name. "Why in the world would you value the advice of some deputy sheriff who lives in a place like Winter Break over the concerns of your own parents?"

I poured a big cup of coffee then plopped down on the stool next to her. "What do you mean when you say, 'a place like Winter Break'? I love this town and the people who live here. There's nothing wrong with Winter Break, Kansas. Frankly, your comment sounds absolutely snobbish. What if I asked you and Daddy why you'd live in 'a place like China'? Would that offend you?"

My mother rolled her eyes and sighed. "China and Winter Break are not the least bit comparable, Ivy. Quit trying to change the subject. It's clear to me that you're not safe here. First Bitty is murdered, and now someone is threatening you."

I fought to contain the growing resentment that nibbled viciously at me. I wanted to remind my mother that I was now an adult and capable of making my own decisions. I also wanted to tell her that it would take a visitation from God for me to believe I wasn't supposed to be in Winter Break, and that I didn't believe the Holy Spirit had vacated His job and given my mother the position. However, I knew that it was my responsibility to honor my parents, and those comments would most probably fall outside the "honor" guidelines. I took a deep breath and let my words come out in measured slowness. "Mother, you and Dad taught me to listen to God's voice. You told me that I should strive to be led by Him. I try to do that every day. I truly believe I am supposed to be here. I don't know exactly why, but I'm convinced that one of the reasons has to do with 'some deputy sheriff,' as you called him."

Mom started to say something, but I hushed her. "Listen, Mother. Let's give this a rest, okay? We went over this same ground last night so many times, I think I've memorized the entire debate. I'm not leaving. I'm sorry it upsets you; I really am. I'd like to think you were happy about the life I've found in Winter Break. It would be wonderful if you could share in my happiness, but if that's not possible, so be it. I'd like today to be a peaceful day if at all possible. I didn't get much sleep, and I'm probably a little cranky."

My mother took a long sip of her coffee but then stared into her cup for what seemed like an eternity. I steeled myself for whatever new assault was being prepared for launch. I wasn't prepared for her to look up at me and smile.

"What?" I asked, worrying that this was some kind of new tactic designed to throw me off track.

"Oh, Ivy," she said in a soft voice. "I was just remembering the argument I had with your grandmother when I told her my heart's desire was to go to China as a missionary. She spouted some of the same things to me that I've been saying to you. And my reply to her was almost word for word what you just said to me." She shook her head slowly. "Why did I forget about that until just this minute?"

She reached over and took my hand. "I really do want you to be in God's perfect will, honey, but I am worried about you. Your father and I pray over you every day, and we believe in God's protection. But you know that even the most cautious of us can open a door to trouble without meaning to. Your Aunt Bitty did that by trusting someone she shouldn't have. I need to be certain that's not what's happening here."

"I understand that, Mother, I really do. But I *do* belong in Winter Break. And as far as the letter last night and the things that have been happening, I believe I've been given an opportunity to solve a mystery that might restore a son to his mother. Whether Bert Bird is alive or dead, I'd like Ruby to finally be able to lay his disappearance to rest. It's obvious that someone thinks I can do it, and believed it enough to have sent me this warning."

"And tried to burn down the bookstore," my mother added.

I nodded. "There's something strange going on, and I think I'm close to the answer."

"You said you want to help Ruby find closure, but how do you know she doesn't already know where Bert is?"

"I don't know that, but my gut reaction tells me that her cover story about relatives isn't true. If you'd seen her reaction to the sight of Bert's lunch box and the things inside it, you wouldn't believe it either. Ruby misses her son. I'm sure of it. Something else is going on. And even if Ruby does know where he is, and I doubt it, *I* want to know what happened to Bert Bird. Someone's gone to a lot of trouble to keep his whereabouts secret. I want to know why."

My mother got up and refilled our coffee cups. "Okay, Ivy," she said, sitting down next to me and handing me my cup, "why don't you start from the beginning? Tell me everything. Maybe I can help."

By the time Amos knocked on the front door, I'd recounted the entire story, from finding the map up to the discovery of the letter the night before. This time, I didn't leave out anything. Although my mother didn't say a word throughout my long-winded discourse, I could tell she was chewing things over in her mind. It was great to feel as if we were actually working together on something, but I still had to wonder if our sudden bonding experience wasn't going to end up causing me some kind of grief.

Amos was looking at the letter when my father burst through the front door. "Amos?" he yelled out. "Amos, where are you?"

"I'm in here, Mickey," Amos said loudly enough for him to hear.

When my father entered the kitchen, it was obvious to all of us that he was upset.

"Mickey," my mother said, "what in the world is wrong?"

My father's usually serene features were tight with anger. He directed his attention to Amos, ignoring my mother and me. "Some crazy fools ran me off the road," he said, his voice quivering with rage. "This nut was tailgating me even though I was going the speed limit. Then he decides to pass me in a no-passing lane. He takes off to go around me with some yahoo driving a truck full of cattle following him. They couldn't possibly have seen what was coming up over the hill. Sure enough, as they sped past me, a big semi was coming toward them in the other lane. I was sure they were going to hit, so I put my car in the ditch to get out of the way."

"Oh, Mickey," my mother said, jumping up and grabbing my father. "Are you okay?"

"I'm fine," my father grumbled. "Just a bit shaken up. I checked the car over, and it looks okay, too, but I certainly put some angels to the test out there."

I ran over and hugged him. "Oh my goodness, Dad. You could have been seriously hurt!"

"I'm okay, honey. Not any worse for wear."

"So what happened?" Amos asked. "Was there an accident?"

"No, it was a miracle someone didn't get hurt. The first guy sped up and made it into the other lane before the semi reached him, and the cattle truck pulled back into my lane. It was a good thing I drove off the road, though, or he would have hit me."

"This just happened?" Amos asked, pulling his

notebook out of his pocket.

He was now in deputy sheriff mode. I liked it when he acted all official. Not just because I was proud of him, but more important, because he was really just too cute for words.

"Yes," my dad said. "I turned around and came back. There can't be a drop of gas left in that car."

"Can you describe both of the trucks?" Amos said, scribbling in his notepad.

"Well, the cattle truck was pretty rickety. It was painted a dark green, but there were gray patches on the hood and the doors. You know, like the primer that goes on before a paint job. The other truck was a regular pickup truck. Newer. Red. I think it was a Ford, but I'm not certain. To be honest, I had my eye on the semi, not the truck."

Amos lowered his notebook and stared at me with an odd expression. Then he turned his attention back to my father. "A red Ford truck?" he asked slowly. "Mickey, this is very important. Did this truck have an extended cab?"

"Sorry," my father said. "I'm not a truck person. You'll have to explain what you mean."

"Did it look like there was more than just a front seat?" Amos asked patiently. "Were there small windows behind the driver's side window?"

My father thought for a few moments. "Now that you mention it," he said slowly, "there were two windows behind the main side window. I hadn't thought about it until now, but I saw the windows as the guy passed me."

Amos's excitement was beginning to show. "Did you happen to notice if there was a metal running board along the side?"

Again my father contemplated Amos's question. Finally, he shook his head. "Sorry, Amos. I just don't remember. It seems to me that there was, but everything happened so quickly, I can't say for sure."

"Dad," I interjected, "did you see the driver of the red pickup?"

He shook his head. "No, his windows were tinted. To be honest, I was more focused on where the truck was than I was on the driver."

"Then we can't be sure it wasn't Odie," I said to Amos.

To my surprise, he grinned at me. "Actually, we can," he said. "I took your advice, Ivy. I went to see Odie. I told him that I believed he was innocent."

"But how does that prove. . . ?"

"It proves it because I just left him at Ruby's," he said excitedly. "We had breakfast together. Odie couldn't have been the one on the highway because he was with me."

"Oh, Amos," I said. "It really isn't Odie! I'm so relieved!"

He held out his arms, and I almost flew into them. "Sounds like you were having some trouble believing the best about Odie, too."

I laughed and pulled back. "Who, me? Nah. I believed in him the whole time."

"Mickey," Amos said, "will you come with me to look for these guys? I think they're the ones who've been stealing cattle all over the county. I'd like to catch them if we could."

"Sure, I'd love to throw a rope around those yahoos. Let's go!"

Amos planted a kiss on my cheek. "I'll talk to you about the note when I get back," he said. "For now, you stay here with your mother. Don't leave the house." He looked toward Mom, who nodded her agreement. Then he and my father hurried out the front door.

"You mentioned someone named Odie," my mother said. "Did you mean Odie Rimrucker?"

I turned and went back into the kitchen. "Yes. I didn't know you knew him."

My mother motioned toward the French doors in the dining room. "Let's finish our coffee outside, okay?"

We stepped out onto the patio, the brisk morning air enveloping us with scented arms of honeysuckle. The rising sun sparkled on the lake while a flock of Canada geese lazily bobbed on the water near the shore. We made ourselves comfortable in the soft wicker patio chairs with their beautiful tropical-colored cushions.

My mother suddenly seemed a million miles away. There was obviously something on her mind. Finally, she cleared her throat and smiled at me. "Since we're being so honest with each other this morning, I'm going to tell you something you don't know. Something that may surprise you. Years and years ago, before I met your father, I was in love with Odie Rimrucker."

She could have told me that she and my father found me in a crater caused by a crashed spaceship from the planet Krypton, and it wouldn't have shocked me as much as this revelation. I couldn't seem to frame any kind of response. Chubby old Odie Rimrucker? Odorous Odie, the town drunk? My mother and this uneducated. . .although I didn't like the connotation the word provided, the only word that came to mind was. . .hick.

Sensing my total confusion, Mom laughed lightly. "You young people seem to think the rest of us were born old, but that isn't true. You see, you're not the only person who used to come to Winter Break during holidays. I spent several summers here as a girl." Her expression became dreamy. "Aunt Bitty and I used to be very close. Why do you think I sent you here so often? I wanted you to enjoy Bitty's companionship the same way I had."

"I—I don't remember you telling me that you'd spent any time here except when you brought me to Winter Break or picked me up." I tried to remember if Bitty had mentioned it. I could remember her talking about my mother with a note of sadness in her voice. At the time, I hadn't paid much attention. Or perhaps I just didn't care. I wouldn't admit this to my mother, but coming to Winter Break had meant trying to forget about her for a while.

"I didn't bring it up much," she said softly, gazing out at the lake. "Probably because I didn't want to think about Odie—and this place." She took a long sip of coffee and then put her cup on the glass table in front of us. "The truth is, I left Odie and Winter Break behind after the summer we broke up. A few years later, I met your dad, and my whole life changed. I put the past in the past and moved on." She shook her head slowly. "Or at least I thought I had. Now I'm beginning to wonder."

"But, Mother, Odie? I—I can't imagine. . ."

She smiled at me, the sides of her mouth quivering in amusement. "If you ever get the chance to look at a picture of Odie Rimrucker when he was a teenager, take it. You'll see a strong, handsome young man with a smile that could melt your heart. It's true that he wasn't as well educated as I was. His grammar left a lot to be desired, but he was romantic, intelligent, and very, very sweet."

I was listening intently, but a vision of my life as the daughter of Odie Rimrucker was tap-dancing through my brain. And it wasn't pretty. I pushed the unflattering picture out of my consciousness and into a dark closet in my mind where, hopefully, it would never escape. "So what happened, Mother?" I asked.

"Unfortunately, Odie's problems with alcohol began early," my mother said sadly. "His father was a raging drunk who beat him and his mother, and although

Odie swore he would never become like his father, he was drawn to the bottle. In the end, he gave in. His choice tortured him, and he drank even more. It was an endless cycle."

"A stronghold," I said, remembering a sermon in which Pastor Taylor had addressed the subject.

My mother nodded. "That's right, Ivy. There was a spiritual stronghold of alcohol in that family. Even though Odie resisted it, the power of it was too strong for him, and he lost his battle." My mother sighed and crossed her arms across her chest as if trying to warm herself. "Of course, I didn't realize it then. I blamed him for being weak. And I left." She looked up at me, and I was surprised to see tears in her eyes. "I left him to deal with it alone."

"It got really bad, Mom," I said. "Eventually Odie lost his family because of it."

"I know." She wiped her eyes with the back of her hand. "Bitty kept me up to date. She knew how much I cared for him."

Something suddenly became clear to me. The story I'd heard about Aunt Bitty nursing Odie through his last and almost fatal bender made sense. "Is that why Bitty took him in when he almost died? Because of you?"

My mother's smile was sad and wistful. "I think Bitty would probably have helped him anyway; that's the kind of person she was. But the answer to your question is yes. When I heard about his situation, I asked her to help him if she could."

"But you and Daddy were married by then."

My mother put her hand up to shield her eyes from the sun, which was beginning to peek over the patio roof. "I never stopped caring about him, Ivy. Not having a romantic relationship with someone doesn't mean you automatically stop being concerned about him. Your father knew all about it. We prayed for Odie together."

The idea of my father praying for my mother's old boyfriend was another shock to my already battered system. I decided right there and then that I didn't really know my parents all that well after all. And I still had a lot of growing up to do.

"So right now, Daddy is out trying to catch the real cattle thieves. If he does, he will have helped to exonerate Odie."

"God answers prayers, Ivy," my mother said with a chuckle. "Maybe He's using us to help Odie because we truly care about him."

"And He sent Amos to talk to Odie while Daddy was dealing with the real thieves so Amos would know Odie was innocent."

My mother reached over and touched my hand. "And He used you to put the idea of talking to Odie in Amos's head. Without that, none of this would have worked out the way it did." She squeezed my fingers.

I nodded dumbly. Sometimes God's love and mercy overwhelm me. I felt that way now.

"Remember, faith only works through love," my mother said. "Our prayers for Odie were activated by our love for him." She let go of my hand and leaned back in her chair.

I sat silently, watching the geese chase something around in the water. Finally, I said, "Then God can use my love for Ruby to help her find her son."

"Wrong," my mother said, her voice so soft I could barely hear her. "God can use *our* love to find Ruby's son."

I turned to stare at my mother, the woman I'd thought I had all figured out. "You're going to help me?"

She grinned at me. "Where do you think you got those Nancy Drew skills, missy? I read all those books in Bitty's collection long before you cracked them open."

I was speechless. The geese waddled out of the lake and begin to nibble on the fresh blades of grass sprouting up around the edge of the water. Although geese could glide beautifully on the water, on land their gait was ungainly and awkward. I was pretty sure I knew how they felt. At that moment, I was a goose out of water. This was new territory for me—and for my mother.

"So our next step is to talk to someone who can tell us who else left town around the time Bert disappeared?" my mom asked.

"Yes, that was my plan. Of course, Dewey was here then. I'm hoping he'll be able to remember something helpful."

"Let's go talk to him now. We have no idea when Amos and your father will be back."

"Amos told us to stay put," I said.

My mother leaned forward in her chair. "Okay.

Then why don't we get Dewey to come here?"

"He's running a store, Mother," I said. "We can't ask him to shut it down because we want to have a chat with him."

She thought for a moment. "Well, he eats lunch, doesn't he? Why not invite him over for lunch?" My mother glanced at her wristwatch. "It's ten thirty now. I could put together some tuna sandwiches and a nice salad."

"I think that would work. He closes from noon to one anyway. I'll call him right now."

By the time Dewey knocked on the front door, my mother had set out a nice meal, even taking time to brew and chill a pitcher of tea, seasoned with a little fresh mint from Marion's yard.

After a few pleasantries, we sat down to lunch on the patio. It was a perfect afternoon. A slight breeze wafted up from the lake, bringing with it a hint of the spring flowers beginning to bloom near the water. I almost hated to say anything that might disrupt nature's gentle ambiance, but those missing bones just wouldn't be still. They called to me.

"Dewey," I said, interrupting a benign conversation about some of the fresh vegetables he would be getting into his store next week. "I need to ask you some questions about Bert Bird. Do you mind?"

He wiped his mouth with his napkin and shook his head. "I was wondering about the real reason you two lovely women asked me to lunch. I'd hoped it was because you couldn't do without my sparkling personality and scintillating conversation."

I grinned at him. "Of course that was the main reason, but I must admit to a small ulterior motive."

Although Dewey and I had no secrets from each other, our morning breakfast meetings had been disrupted, and things had happened that I hadn't had time to tell him. I brought him up to speed about the fire, the lunch box, the bones, and even the warning note. My mother frowned at me when I mentioned the mysterious letter shoved under my front door, but as I said, I had no secrets from Dewey.

When I finished, Dewey sat back in his chair and folded his arms. His forehead was knotted with concern. "I've been wondering about Bert Bird for a long time. I never could figure out why he didn't come back. After a few years, I quit believing he was really living with relatives. He loved it here. And he loved his mother. It was such a mystery." He shook his head slowly. "To be honest with you, at one time I even suspected Ruby of doing away with him." He chuckled. "Of course, after I got to know her better, I knew that wasn't true."

"Was there anyone else you suspected?" I asked.

He took a drink and put his glass down. "Nope. There wasn't anyone in town that had anything against that boy. He was a great kid. I led the Boy Scout troop he was in." He got a faraway look in his eyes. "After his dad died, Bert became almost like a son to me. I mean, he had no father and I didn't have children. I guess we kind of bonded."

"If Bert wasn't planning on coming back," my mother said, "wouldn't he have told you?"

He smiled at her. "You just hit the nail on the head, Margie. That's one thing that still bothers me." His eyes narrowed. "Either we weren't as close as I thought, or something bad happened to that boy."

"And there's the lunch box, Dewey. Someone told me that if he buried it, it was because he knew he *was* coming back. He wouldn't have left something he referred to as *his treasure* if he knew he'd never see it again."

"That sounds right. Of course, we didn't know anything about the lunch box back then."

"I'm curious about something else. Do you remember any of Ruby's relatives coming to pick Bert up? I know it was a long time ago."

"Nope. That's another strange thing. One day he was just gone. If I'd have actually seen someone come for him, I probably wouldn't have been so suspicious of Ruby's story down through the years."

"Dewey," my mother said, "can you remember anyone else who left town around the same time Bert did? Ivy and I wonder if he might have traveled out of town with someone who was leaving Winter Break. At his age, he surely wasn't traveling alone."

He sat back in his chair with a sigh. "It's been a long, long time, but let me see. Well, there was Edith Bruenwalder, but that had nothing to do with Bert.

Edith just had enough of Harvey and took off to live with her sister in Topeka." Dewey's bushy silver eyebrows worked together as he tried to pull up memories from the past. "There were the Carvers. Ben and Tillie were the parents. They had two girls. . .Margaret and. . .what was that other one? Something like RaeAnne. . .can't quite remember. Ben got a job in Nebraska somewhere. I remember when they left because they had an account in the store that needed to be settled first. Ruby owed some, too, although I had no intention of collecting it. This was after Albert died and Ruby was really struggling. Ben asked about her account and offered to pay it. 'Course, almost all the townspeople were pitching in to help her. It's too bad it wasn't enough to keep Bert here. Oh, and there were a couple of Baumgartner kids that took off." He shrugged. "That happens from time to time. Being a Baumgartner is a hard life. I wish I could remember their names, but I just can't at the moment."

The Baumgartner family now numbered in the seventies due to new marriages and brand-new children and grandchildren. Almost all of them lived and worked south of town and attended the First Mennonite Church. It was originally founded by Baumgartners, and elder Baumgartners were dedicated to keeping it going. However, down through the years, a rebellious Baumgartner escaped once in a while. The wayward lambs either disappeared forever or repented and came back to the fold. There were a few exceptions. My friend

Emily was allowed to attend Faith Community Church since she was married to a member. But in her family's eyes, she was now and always would be a Baumgartner. The family certainly wasn't mean-spirited or tyrannical. They were some of the nicest people you'd ever want to meet. But they were dedicated to their church—and their family. Kind of in that order.

"You can't remember either one of them, Dewey?" I asked.

"Wait a minute. Emily's mother was one of them. But of course, she came back." He drew his eyebrows together once again. "Right now I just can't remember who the other one was. But I don't think he ever returned. It was a boy as I recall. Darrel? Darrin?" He shook his head. "Inez would recollect it, since he left about the same time. I'm just not sure."

Inez was Emily's mother. That would be easy enough to check out. Inez had always liked me. She was almost like a second mother to me when I was young. I remembered that Emily had already mentioned getting together sometime this week. Maybe we could meet for coffee. I made a mental note to call her later today and set up a time to get together.

"Was there anyone else, Dewey?" my mother asked.

He sighed. "Sorry. That's all I can remember. There haven't been that many people in and out of Winter Break over the years, so that's liable to be about it. Of course, I can't be completely sure any of these people left exactly when Bert did. I could be off some. Trying to recall something that happened thirty years ago isn't that easy." He shook his head. "You really think this will help you figure out what happened to Bert?"

I shrugged. "I have no idea, Dewey, but say a prayer for me. I'm running out of ideas."

"You know, there is someone you should talk to," he said. "Bonnie Peavey."

"I intend to. I'm just waiting for a chance to get her alone. She's always with Ruby."

Dewey nodded. "I've never told anyone this before, but I'm going to tell you, Ivy. Bert and Bonnie were about as crazy about each other as any two people have ever been. I saw them together quite a bit because they'd come in the store to buy candy after school. But Bonnie's family wouldn't have put up with her having a boyfriend, and Ruby would have blown her stack if she'd known Bert was making goo-goo eyes at Bonnie. Ruby and Bonnie's mother didn't get along. In my opinion, Bonnie Peavey knows as much as anyone about what happened to Bert Bird."

I thanked Dewey for his help before he headed back to the store. My next move would be to talk to Bonnie Peavey.

14

It was almost nine o'clock that night before we heard from Amos and my father. When they finally ambled through the front door, there was a look of satisfaction on their faces.

"You got them?" I asked with anticipation.

Amos grinned slowly and slapped my father on the back. "Thanks to your dad, the cattle thieves are behind bars this evening. We even recovered some of the cattle. A couple of lowlifes out of Richfield were working together to steal cows and sell them to a guy in Dodge City who didn't care if they were branded or not."

"That's great. Does Odie know?"

"Not yet," Amos said. "But he's about to." He strolled into the library, where there was a phone and a little privacy.

I was thrilled that he'd told Odie he believed in him before the real thieves were caught. Now Odie would never think that Amos's words came as a result of the capture. At least that situation was behind us.

"Well, I guess your old boyfriend is in the clear, Margie," Dad said. "God answers prayers."

"Yes, He does," my mother said, giving my father a big hug. "And you're living proof of that."

Although I hadn't expected to feel this way when

I found out my parents were coming to Winter Break, I was suddenly really glad they were here. I'd almost forgotten how great they could be.

My dad mentioned that he and Amos hadn't gotten a chance to eat all evening, so my mother and I fixed them sandwiches and fruit. I'd just cut Amos's sandwich in half when he came around the corner after talking to Odie. The smile on his face told me everything I needed to know.

"Thanks again for your advice, Ivy," he said. "I'm glad this is over as far as Odie is concerned." Even though he seemed relieved, the look on his face still held an uneasiness.

"Is something else bothering you?" I asked.

Amos studied the pattern in the rug as if something was written there. Finally, he looked up. "These guys we picked up don't seem like they have enough sense to put together something like this. I have to wonder if someone else is pulling the strings. Someone who set this up and used them to carry out his plan."

"Why don't you eat something and think about it later," I said. "You and Dad need to relax for a while and celebrate your victory. I'm just grateful you're both all right."

"Except for the ten years those cattle thieves took off my life," my dad grumbled.

"Now, Mickey," my mother said, "don't say things like that. I plan for you to be around a long, long time." She handed him his plate, and he sat down at the bar to eat. Then she put her arms around his neck and kissed the top of his head. "I have to have someone to boss around, you know."

My dad sighed. "I know. It's my cross to bear."

Amos and I laughed. The thought entered my mind that I hoped I would be as happily married someday as my parents were. Without thinking, I glanced over at Amos. I was surprised to find him looking at me with an odd expression. We both turned our eyes away quickly, but I could feel a warm flush spread across my face. I looked down at my feet, hoping my face would tone itself down a few shades before anyone noticed. I couldn't help but wonder what Amos was thinking. Surely we hadn't been turning over the same idea in our heads. I couldn't help but remember that he'd said he had a question to ask me. I didn't want to get my hopes up.

The truth was, I had no idea if Amos was even interested in getting married. I could still remember the pain he suffered when his folks got divorced. "I'm never getting married," he'd said tearfully. "It just doesn't work." Of course, that happened a long time ago, when he was just a kid. I hoped he didn't still feel the same way.

My dad's booming voice broke my reverie. "Let's all get some sleep. This has been an exciting day. I'm taking everyone out for breakfast in the morning. Ruby's hotcakes and sausage for me!" I glanced over at my mother, but to her credit, she just smiled at me and nodded.

I grabbed Amos's arm. "I'll walk you out," I said.

After Amos said his good-byes to my parents, we strolled out into a cool, star-filled night. The cicadas sang to us, and the full moon shone down, highlighting the budding trees that surrounded the house and lined the road back to town.

"I love this house," I said softly. "I've always wanted to live here. It's been wonderful, even if it's almost time to leave."

Amos smacked his forehead. "Oh, shoot. With everything going on, I totally forgot. I ran into Milton today. He said you should be able to open up the bookstore on Saturday. Almost everything is done. They're just waiting for the spackling to dry so they can paint the walls. They'll finish that tomorrow. After a day of letting the place air out, you're good to go."

I breathed a sigh of relief. "I'm so glad and so thankful for everyone who pitched in to help." I grabbed his hand. "Let's throw a party to thank everyone, okay? We could have it here—just like one of the parties Marion used to throw. We'll pull out Cecil's old grill and fix hot dogs and hamburgers. The kids could swim in the lake. What do you think?"

"Well, I think it would be best to call Cecil and Marion to see if they'd mind, but I think it's a wonderful idea," he said. "I'll be glad to help."

I laughed. "As if Cecil and Marion would say no. They loved throwing parties here. I bet they'll be thrilled."

He turned to leave but hesitated on the last step. "Ivy," he said in a tone so low I had to strain to hear him. "I. . .I'm. . .I mean, I. . ." He swung around and stared at me. I was shocked to see tears shining in his eyes. "Never mind," he whispered. "We'll talk about it some other time."

"What is it, Amos? Is something wrong?"

"No. No, everything's fine. We need to talk about something, but this isn't the time." He pulled on his hat and strode toward the patrol car without looking back at me. As he drove away, I couldn't help but wonder what was bothering him. Things were going so well, surely there wasn't a problem with our relationship. Just a few minutes ago I was thinking about what it would be like to marry Amos, and now I was feeling insecure. I pushed away the worry that wanted to burrow down and get comfortable in my psyche before it took root. It was ridiculous. Amos and I were fine. We'd deal with whatever was on his mind when he was ready to discuss it. When I went back inside the house, I almost missed seeing my mother, who sat silently at the breakfast bar, staring at me.

"Is everything all right?" she asked, looking concerned.

I guess my expression hadn't caught up to my resolve. "Yes. Sure," I said, trying to sound as upbeat as possible. I had no intention of airing out my love life right now. No matter how well my mother and I were getting along.

"We need to talk to Bonnie," she said. The abrupt change in conversation threw me.

"What?"

She frowned and shot me one of those looks mothers perfect so well. It always made me feel that she was wondering if I was really her child—or whether she might have picked up the wrong package at the hospital.

"Bonnie Peavey," she said slowly so I could grasp the complicated concept.

"Oh, right." The stress and excitement of the day were beginning to take their toll on me. I was mentally wiped out. "It will be impossible to talk to her during the morning rush. We'll have to find a way to get her alone."

"She smokes," my mother said. "I saw her hiding behind the restaurant the other day with a cigarette. We'll just wait until she goes outside; then we'll go out there and talk to her."

I wasn't crazy about the idea of standing anywhere near cigarette smoke, but if I could find a place upwind, it would be a good time to trap Bonnie without everyone in town listening to our conversation.

"Sounds good, Mother," I said. "But I'm exhausted. I'm going upstairs to bed. Let's take this up in the morning."

"Is everything all right, Ivy? You look worried. Are things okay with you and Amos?"

My mother's radar was activated and tracking nicely. "As far as I know, everything's fine," I said. "I'm just beat. I've got to get some sleep."

"Okay, dear," she replied with a smile. "I'll see you

in the morning, bright and early."

It might be early, but right at that moment, I wasn't sure how bright I'd be.

I climbed the stairs to the attic room. After changing my clothes and crawling into bed, I stared up at the pretend stars that glowed on the ceiling. I wanted to lie in bed and think about all the things that were going on, but I remembered Aunt Bitty's advice about piling things on my plate. I decided to hand it over to the One who could actually clean it up, make it sparkle, and hand it back to me full of blessings. Then I drifted off into a peaceful sleep.

The next morning, I awoke to my mother's gentle prodding. "Wake up, Sleeping Beauty," she whispered into my ear. She'd awakened me the same way every morning when I was little. Now that I was an adult, it seemed childish—but it still made me feel good.

By the time I got downstairs, my parents were ready to go. I'd barely swallowed two gulps of coffee before we were out the door. As I started down the drive, my dad went over the events of the previous evening for about the third time. The excitement in his voice made me smile, but I was hoping this would be the last go-round. His eyes shone as he described the feeling of racing after the bad guys. Although I was pretty sure my mother wanted to chew him out for getting himself in the middle of a dangerous situation, she kept quiet. She was allowing him to have his moment in the sun. I knew her well enough to know that he was scheduled for a serious talking-to in the near future.

We turned off the long path from the house onto the road that led into town. On the way, we passed several farmhouses. However, I saw something at Homer Wilson's house that made me stop and pull up to the driveway. Lucy Barber's SUV was parked at the end of the drive, and its back door was wide open.

"I'll be right back," I said to my surprised parents.

I crept up slowly to the SUV, keeping my eye on Homer's front door. There was no gas can anywhere to be found in the back of the vehicle. I tiptoed around to the side. Near the backseat, lying on the floor, was something that took my breath away. I felt dizzy for a moment, but when I realized that at any second Lucy could come out and find me inspecting her car, I turned and ran back to where my parents waited with inquisitive expressions.

"What are you doing?" my mother asked as soon as I slid back behind the wheel. I pulled away as slowly as I could. Driving on gravel roads is a noisy business, and I didn't want to draw attention to myself.

When we were well away from Homer's house, I pulled the car over. Before I could get a word out, she said, "Ivy, you look like you've seen a ghost. What in the world is going on?"

"It was in her car, Mother. But it doesn't make sense—"

"What was in her car, Ivy? What are you talking about?" My mother's stern tone shook me out of my stupor.

"The barrel tapper," I said slowly. "Lucy Barber has a barrel tapper in her SUV."

My father, who had been listening patiently to our conversation, interrupted. "What are you two talking about? What's a barrel tapper?"

I reminded him that it was the same device that Amos had already described in Harvey's orchard when we were looking for a nonexistent body.

"So what's so funny about the lady doctor having one of her own?" he asked in a grumpy voice. "You can't tell me that there's only one of those silly things in the whole world. Out in this neck of the woods, there must be lots of them."

"I don't think so, Dad. They're not that common. Besides, it looked like the exact one I found marking the body in the orchard."

"But, Ivy," my mother chimed in, "your dad has a point. There's no way to tell if it's the same one. Are you certain you saw it clearly? Maybe it was something else—something that reminded you of the instrument you saw."

I was certain about what I'd seen—until my mother managed to put doubts in my mind. I would have to look again—but more closely this time. I needed to remove the tapper from Lucy's SUV. Instead of gazing at it through smoky, dark glass, I wanted to hold it in my hands and make certain it was the tapper that had been used to indicate Bert's grave.

Of course, thinking that Lucy was somehow involved in Bert's death was ludicrous. She wasn't even alive when he disappeared. But why did she have the tapper? Did she know who killed him—and who moved the body? Was she involved somehow?

These questions bumped around in my head until I couldn't think straight. And I still didn't have any answers.

We pulled up to Ruby's a few minutes later. Amos's patrol car was already parked outside. When we got inside, I spotted him in a booth next to the wall. When he saw us, he waved us over. As we made our way to where he waited, I spotted Emily and Buddy having breakfast.

"Go ahead," I told my parents. "I'll be with you in a minute."

"Hello there, Ivy!" Buddy bellowed as I approached their table. "Looks like you've got the whole crew out for breakfast."

"I wanted to give you a kiss on the cheek, Buddy," I said. I bent over next to him and whispered, "Emily told me the wonderful news. I'm so happy for you."

Buddy's grin nearly split his face in two. "Thanks, Ivy," he said softly. "And thanks for keeping it to yourself until we can make the official announcement. Emily couldn't stand to keep it from you. I'm glad she has someone she trusts so much."

"I am, too," I said, patting his broad shoulder.

I turned my attention to the beaming mother-to-be. "Emily, I want to ask you a favor. I'm trying to find out who left town around the time Bert Bird disappeared. I heard your mother may have gone away for a while right around the same time. She might remember someone else who left either in the weeks before or after Bert went missing. Could you ask her for me?"

"Sure, Ivy," she said. "I'd be happy to." A frown colored her perfect features. "I didn't know Mother

ever left Winter Break. This is the first I've heard of
it." She reached over and touched my arm. "I'll dig
up some information for you, Sherlock, if you'll meet
me here for coffee this afternoon." She smiled at me.
"I won't keep you long—not so long that your parents
would be offended. But long enough for you to get
what I imagine is a much-needed break."

I grinned back at her. "You know me too well, you
know that? I was going to suggest the very same thing."
I glanced over at my parents, who smiled broadly.
"What time?"

"How about three o'clock?" Emily said.

I leaned down and kissed her cheek. "I'll be here."

My parents sat together on one side of the booth.
I slid in next to Amos, who didn't bother to greet me.
He was focused on the menu written on the dry-erase
board at the front of the restaurant.

My mother kicked me under the table when
Bonnie appeared next to us with her order pad. I
shook my head at her. Ruby was flying around the
room. There wasn't any way to talk to Bonnie now. I
ended up ordering only coffee and toast, and I wasn't
certain I could even get that down. I had butterflies in
my stomach from the discovery in Lucy's SUV. There
wasn't a lot of room left for food.

After Bonnie walked away, I leaned closer to Amos.
"I thought you'd like to know that I might have found
the barrel tapper this morning," I said quietly.

"What?" Amos said.

"The barrel tapper. I think I know where it is."

His confused look told me he'd forgotten about it. "The barrel tapper that marked the place where Bert's box was buried—along with a slightly missing body?"

"Oh, yeah. Sorry," he said sheepishly. "I was thinking about something else."

"Sorry to disturb you," I said sarcastically. "I just thought you might like to know who has an item that was taken when the body was removed from its burial site."

"She found it in Lucy Barber's car," my mother blurted out, stealing my thunder.

His mouth dropped open. "I don't believe it. Why would she have it?"

"Well, that's the sixty-four-thousand-dollar question, isn't it?" I said. "It doesn't make any sense unless she was in the orchard. But why would Lucy Barber move Bert's body? Lucy only started working in Winter Break a couple of years ago. She couldn't possibly have known Bert Bird. Even if she'd lived near Winter Break all her life, she wasn't even born when he left." I sighed. "You know, the more clues we get, the more confusing this whole thing is."

"Ivy, you keep saying that the body in the orchard is Bert Bird," my dad interjected. "But you have no way of knowing that, do you?"

"No," I said, "but he's the only one missing."

"Not necessarily," Amos said. "Maybe it was someone else."

"Maybe," I said. "The only thing we know for sure

is that *someone* was buried there, and it wasn't an animal. No one would have gone to so much trouble to move a dead cow."

"I think you're right," my mother said, "but Amos has a point. What if it's someone completely different? Someone who disappeared years later—or earlier than the time you're concerned with?"

I shook my head. "Unless someone else buried Bert's lunch box after he left, the body had to be placed there first. Either Bert buried his box on top of the body, or someone buried Bert Bird and his box at the same time. Bert is the key to this mystery. If we can find out what happened to him, we'll figure out the rest of the story." I sighed and put my head in my hands. "Hopefully we'll get the answers we're looking for sometime in my lifetime."

Bonnie came back with Amos's orange juice and a carafe of coffee for the rest of us. As she poured coffee into my cup, I looked around for Ruby. She was at the cash register, ringing up customers. I made a quick decision. "Bonnie," I said, keeping my voice low, "I need to talk to you. In private. It's about Bert Bird. I need to ask you some questions about what happened when he left Winter Break."

It's a good thing I have fast reflexes. Bonnie almost lost her grip on the carafe, and coffee spilled right where I'd been resting my arm.

"I–I'm sorry," she sputtered. "Are you all right?"

"Yes, I'm okay. Please don't worry about it." I used

my napkin to wipe up the mess before it dripped down on my jeans.

Bonnie's eyes darted quickly toward the front of the room—to where Ruby stood talking to a customer. "Come by tonight," she said in a low voice. "After we close. I always stay late and lock up. Come around ten." She glanced once again toward Ruby. "But if *she's* here, keep going. She can't know that I'm talking to you."

"All right, Bonnie. I'll be here."

She turned on her heel and swept past us.

"I'm coming with you," my mother whispered.

I shook my head. "Bonnie doesn't know you, Mom," I said. "It would be better if I came by myself."

"I'll drive you," Amos said. "With the way things have been going, I want to be nearby in case something else happens." I started to argue with him, but he shook his head. "It's not negotiable, Ivy. I'll park around the side of the building. Bonnie will never know I'm here."

"Thanks, Amos," my dad said. "That will make me feel better."

My mother wasn't saying anything, but I knew she was upset. I reached over and patted her hand. "I promise, I'll rush home after I talk to Bonnie and tell you every single thing we talked about, okay?"

She smiled. "Okay, as long as you don't leave anything out."

"I won't. I promise."

Our conversation was suddenly interrupted by someone speaking loudly. I immediately recognized the voice. Three tables away from us, Bertha and Delbert Pennypacker were giving Bonnie their breakfast order.

"I'll have the steak and eggs, please," Bertha said in a shrill voice. "And make certain that steak is medium, will you, please? The last time we were here, my steak was terribly overcooked." She batted her eyes and glanced around the room to see if anyone was paying any attention to her. I turned my head so she wouldn't think I was listening. I noticed that most of the other people in the restaurant were also ignoring her.

Delbert seemed to be looking at his place mat intently. When he finally ordered, he barely acknowledged Bonnie—or his wife. Although Delbert Pennypacker had a reputation for being lazy, drinking too much, and chasing other women, I almost felt sorry for him. I couldn't imagine what life with Bertha had to be like. The thought made me shiver.

While my dad made small talk with Amos, I tried to piece together all the confusing facts that surrounded the missing Bert Bird. It reminded me of a hot, lazy summer afternoon years ago, when Emily and I tried to put together one of her mother's huge puzzles. We worked on that thing for hours, but we couldn't get more than a few of the pieces to fit. When Inez came home and found us, she burst out laughing.

"Oh no, girls," she'd said. "I dumped three different puzzles that were missing pieces into that box. I was going to throw them away!"

I felt the same way now, as if I were trying to piece

together one picture but there were too many pieces that didn't match. Maybe my meeting with Bonnie would help me to see the final image a little more clearly.

While my father recounted some story about the difficulty of finding good American food in China, I chewed on my dry toast and tried to ignore Amos as he shoveled mounds of Ruby's stuffed French toast into his mouth. The incredible aroma made my stomach rumble. Watching him consume forkfuls of hot berries and cream cheese tucked into Ruby's homemade bread, which had been baked in butter and covered in real maple syrup, made me feel as if I were trying to ingest cardboard.

Maybe it was my decision to look away from the gastric performance playing itself out next to me or maybe it was just God nudging my head in the right direction, but my eye caught something that made me choke on my toast.

Amos's slapping me on the back and my mother's trying to get me to take a drink of water made it more than a little difficult to talk, but I finally was able to sputter, "I'm okay. I'm okay! Quit hitting me!"

"Are you sure you're all right, punkin?" my dad asked in a worried tone.

I coughed a few more times, gave Amos a dirty look for his overenthusiastic beating, and croaked out, "The letter. I know who wrote the letter warning me to stop looking for Bert Bird."

16

I wish you'd just left things alone. It won't do no good to dig up the past this way. Bert is gone, and it's for the best."

Amos, my parents, and I sat in the empty restaurant alone with Ruby. After I'd confronted her, telling her I realized the handwriting on the note matched the scrawled menu items on her large dry-erase board, she'd promised to talk to us after the morning rush. We waited for people to eat their fill and then head back home or out to the fields. Finally, around ten thirty, Ruby shooed the last of the "lollygaggers," as she called them, out the front door. She locked it and turned the CLOSED sign around to prevent further interruptions. Then she reluctantly joined us at our table.

"Ruby," Amos said, "there's still a missing body out there. I can't look the other way because you tell me to. You know that. You've got to tell me the truth. What happened to Bert?"

Ruby pulled a chair up next to our booth. Her wrinkled face sagged with weariness, and her eyes were full of long-held pain. "I don't know nothin' 'bout a body, Deputy," she said in a tired voice. "You see, my Bert ain't dead as far as I know."

"You. . .you know Bert's alive?" I said. "Where is he?"

She shook her head, her platinum wig jiggling like

it had a mind of its own and was in complete agreement with its ancient owner. "I have no idea where my boy is. I haven't known for a long, long time."

"Why don't you start at the beginning," my mother said soothingly. "We'll just hush and let you tell the story your way."

Ruby flashed her a grateful look. "Thank you, Margie. I believe that would be the best way to go." She took a deep breath and blew it out. "First of all, let me say that I'm plumb sorry I wrote you that note, Ivy." She looked at me with tearful eyes. "At the time I wrote it, it sounded okay to me. But the more I thought about it, the more I realized you might have thought I was threatenin' you in some way." A tear spilled from one of her red-rimmed eyes and splashed down on her careworn cheek. "Nothing could be further from the truth. I appreciate you findin' Bert's stuff, and I appreciate the way you care about him—and me. But I can't have you lookin' for him. He was the one I was talkin' about in that note. The one I was afraid would wind up hurt."

Ruby took the edge of her apron and wiped her eyes. Then she breathed a sigh that seemed to come from somewhere deep inside her soul. "Before I tell you what happened to my Bert, I have to ask you to keep what I'm about to tell you to yourselves. It wouldn't do no good for folks to know."

While the rest of us mumbled our agreement, Amos kept quiet. Ruby stared at him with one eyebrow raised. "I didn't hear nothin' from you, Amos Parker."

"I can't make that promise, Ruby," he said. "You know that. If there's foul play. . ."

"Ain't no foul play, Deputy," she answered. "Not the legal kind, anyway."

"If that's true, you have my word, as well," Amos said. "I'll keep your secret if I possibly can."

That appeared to satisfy her. She took another deep, shaky breath. "When Elbert and I came to Winter Break, we had such high hopes. We'd been tryin' to scrape out a livin' in Oklahoma, but it was hard. Elbert was workin' for a man who owned a feed store. He wasn't gettin' paid much in the first place, but then the man started cheatin' him out of money. He blamed Elbert for weighin' the feed wrong. Said it was costin' the store money. His boss would take money out of Elbert's pay, sayin' he was just collectin' what he owed." Even after all these years, Ruby's eyes sparkled with righteous indignation. "Elbert Bird wouldn't take a dime that didn't belong to him. He wouldn't even pick up money dropped in the street. 'Why, Ruby,' he'd say, 'someone might be lookin' for that. Might be all the money they have for dinner. We better let it sit right there so the owner can retrace his steps and find it.' Man like that ain't stealin' anything from anybody. Well, anyways, baby Bert come right around that time. Elbert was tryin' his best to take care of us, but things got harder and harder. Then we got a telegraph from Elbert's uncle Leonard, tellin' us he was sick and askin' us would we please come to Kansas and help run his farm." Ruby smiled. "It was the answer to a prayer. We packed up and came to Winter Break."

She seemed to drift away a little, probably seeing happier times in her mind's eye. Then she shook herself and refocused on her story. "It was tough takin' care of Uncle Leonard, don't get me wrong, but he was a kind man. I truly loved him. It was hard when he passed, but then we found out that he'd left everything to us. We finally had a chance to have somethin' of our own—to turn our lives around in a positive direction. And we did just that." Ruby's smile held a note of pride. "Elbert and me made that place into a right fine dairy farm. The best around. For the first time in our lives, we had everything we needed, and life was good."

The light left Ruby's eyes, and she stared down toward the floor. "Then it happened. Elbert went out one day to tend the cows, and he never came home. I told him not to go out in that lightnin' storm. Somethin' told me he wasn't supposed to be out there, but he wouldn't listen." She wiped her face with her apron again. "I wish like everything I'd insisted he stay inside. I shoulda run out there after him and dragged him back into the house. But I didn't, and he died."

Ruby raised her hand to pat down her wig. Her fingers trembled visibly. "So. . .I was left alone to raise Bert. I tried to keep the farm going, I really did. Bert did everything he could to help me, but I made him go to school. School came first. The farm second."

Ruby shook her head. "I truly believe that boy woulda worked himself into the ground if I'd let him. But I wanted him to be something more than a farmer, depending on the weather and such. I wanted him to have a good job—a better life than Elbert and me."

Ruby grew silent, staring at something across the room. We waited for what seemed like an eternity but was really only a few seconds. Finally, my mother touched Ruby's arm.

"Go on, Ruby," she said gently. "Tell us what happened next."

The old woman's body shuddered. "It's hard to tell this next part. No matter how I say it, it makes me sound like a rotten mother. At the time, though, I thought it was the best thing for Bert." Her pleading gaze seemed to lock onto each one of us, searching for some kind of understanding.

"Go on," my mother said again.

"Our neighbors," Ruby said in a voice so low we all leaned forward to hear her, "Ben and Tillie Carver, were leaving for Nebraska. Ben got a job at a farm implement company as a salesman. It was a good job with good pay. They had two daughters, Margaret and DeAnn. Bert was friends with the girls. They seemed like such a nice family."

Again Ruby paused in her narrative, seemingly reluctant to continue. Finally, she began again. Her voice shook, making it hard to understand her. "Ben Carver offered to take Bert with them to Nebraska for a couple of months. He knew I was having problems and couldn't take care of him properly." She put her head in her hands. "I. . .I thought Bert would be better off gettin' away from here for a while. I didn't want him to worry no more. It was summer and school was out, so it seemed like the perfect solution while I decided what to do." She paused again before raising her head to look at us. Her expression was one of bewilderment. "It was just for a while," she said again. "Until I could sell the farm and make things better for us. Maybe I was wrong, but I didn't know what else to do. It was gettin' so I couldn't keep the boy fed proper."

"Why did you tell everyone Bert was going to stay with family?" my father asked. "You didn't do anything wrong. Why make up a story?"

She shook her head. "Pride," she said slowly. "Nothin' more than stinkin' pride. Everyone in town had been trying to help me out so much, I was too embarrassed to tell them I couldn't care for my own son, even with their help. I figured if I said Bert was stayin' with relatives out of town, no one would ask any questions, and I could concentrate on finding a way out of my problems without havin' to take any more charity."

"What happened, Ruby?" I asked. "Why didn't Bert come back?"

"I promised him, Ivy," she said, tears beginning to make shiny trails down her cheeks. "I promised him I would come for him as soon as I could. I sold the farm, and with the money I made, I opened this restaurant."

A small smile shone through her tears. "I got the idea from Bert. He'd tell me, 'Mama, you are the best cook in the whole world. If you had a restaurant, everyone in town would eat there.' " She wiped her face with her apron. "I remembered him sayin' that, so I bought this building and started cookin'. Sure enough, people started comin' and I began to get ahead a little. Right away, I called the Carvers and told 'em I was coming for Bert. Ben Carver told me that Bert didn't want to come home. That he was happier livin' with them."

"I don't get it," Amos said. "Bert was with them only a few months, right? Why would he say something like that?"

Ruby nodded, her wig jumping up and down. "That's exactly what I wondered," she said. "I knew my boy loved me. Why wouldn't he want to come home? I told them I was comin' to get him anyway. But then I got his letter."

"He sent a letter?" my mother asked. "You didn't actually talk to him?"

Ruby shook her head. "No, Ben said he didn't want to talk to me. He said he wrote down everything he wanted to say."

"What was in the letter, Ruby?" I asked.

She covered her face with her apron for a moment. When she lowered it, I wanted to cry. In all my life, I don't think I'd ever seen so much sorrow in any person's face.

"He said he was happy livin' with the Carvers. That he didn't need me, and he didn't want to live in Winter

Break. That there was lots of things in Nebraska that Winter Break didn't have. He said it would be best if we just left each other alone." Ruby's last words were wrapped around her sobs. She pulled her apron up over her face again, this time crying bitterly into it.

My mother scooted next to her and wrapped her arms around the grieving woman. I reached across the table and put my hand on her arm. There wasn't anything to say. All we could do was try to comfort her.

Finally, her crying lessened and she pulled the apron down. "I couldn't believe it at first," she sputtered. "My Bert wouldn't say those kinds of things to me. After a while, I decided to go to Beatrice—that's where they was livin'—and just make him come home. He was still a boy, and I was his mama. He'd have to come if I made him. But the Carvers were gone. I looked for them for a long time, callin' their relatives and friends, tryin' to find out where they were. I even went to the police in town and asked for their help. They checked around a little, but they couldn't find no sign of them either. After a while I quit lookin'. I decided that if Bert wanted to come home, he knew where I was. He'd been with the Carvers awhile by then. He must have been happier with them than he'd been with me, and I wanted him to be happy more than anything. I been waitin' in Winter Break all these years just in case he changed his mind and came home. But that was thirty-some years ago. He probably has a wife and kids by now. He doesn't want anything to do with me;

that's obvious." She reached over and grabbed my hand. "That's why I pushed that note under your door, Ivy. You're a smart girl. I was afraid you'd uncover the truth and go lookin' for Bert. I know it's easier to find people now, what with the Internet and all, but I don't want to interfere in his life. I don't want to mess him up any more. I'm really sorry about the note," she said. "I truly didn't mean to scare you."

My mother patted Ruby's shoulder. "She understands, Ruby," she said. "Don't worry about it."

Ruby locked her pain-filled eyes on mine. "Will you promise to keep my secret?" she asked in a strained voice. "Will you please just leave this alone now?"

Before I could answer, my mother spoke up again. "Ivy won't look for Bert anymore, Ruby," she said. "I promise."

I was beginning to feel like a puppet with my mother pulling the strings.

"Amos?" Ruby said. "What about you?"

"I'm sorry you've gone through so much, Ruby. Whatever you want to do is fine with me."

"Good. Good," she said with a deep, slow sigh. She slapped her hand on the top of the table. "Now I've got to get things going for the lunch rush. You folks need to head on out of here."

It was as if a strong wind had suddenly swept the past few minutes away. Ruby was her old self. She stood up and headed for her kitchen, ready to go on with life as if nothing had happened, her pain shut behind a door she'd kept closed for many years. Before she reached the door to the kitchen, she stopped and whirled back around.

"I'd still like my boy's lunch box and keepsakes," she said. "It would give me somethin' to remember him by." With that, she was gone. Within seconds, the sounds of chopping came from the kitchen, along with the aroma of jalapeños. Ruby's Redbird Burgers were getting ready to make another appearance. My breakfast of dry toast lay cold and flat in my stomach. I could swear I heard it whispering, "Redbird Burger. Redbird Burger."

"Let's get going," my mother said.

I started to say something, but she shushed me. "Outside," she whispered. Her face was set and angry. I couldn't begin to imagine why. I knew why *I* was hopping mad. My mother had given Ruby a promise I hadn't made. And I still had lots of questions.

When we got outside, my mother turned to me. "Sorry about speaking for you, Ivy," she said. "But I had to get us out of there."

"Something's wrong with Ruby's story," my dad said. "Your mother picked it up, too."

"What do you mean?" Amos asked. "Don't you believe her?"

"Well, first of all," my mother said, "it bothers me that Ruby never got to talk to Bert himself. Who knows why he wrote that letter—or if he even did?"

My dad put his arm around me. "Parents and

children have a bond, Amos. It can't be broken that easily. Even if Bert did want to stay with the Carvers, he should have wanted to visit his mother at least once in the last thirty years. Even kids with lousy parents usually try to mend fences at some point. Something about this whole thing stinks like dead fish left lying in the sun."

Amos had an odd look on his face. He'd tried to reach out to his own father, although his attempt hadn't been successful. Maybe my parents were right.

"Well," I said, "if I'm finally allowed to talk, may I say that you put me in an awful position when you promised Ruby that I was going to leave this alone? I don't think I can do that. I want to find Bert. With the Internet, I'll bet—"

"Ivy," my mother said, "I only said that so that Ruby wouldn't put the rest of us on the spot. *I* didn't promise anything. I intend to do exactly what you said. Look for Bert Bird online. If he's listed in any phone book in the nation, we'll find him."

"Why, Mother," I said. "How delightfully devious of you. And you being a missionary and all. . ."

"There are many facets to your old mother, my dear," she said. "The detective side of me has been awakened."

"May I suggest to you and Dr. Watson," my dad said, "that we continue this conversation somewhere else. Ruby might get suspicious if she sees us out here jabbering."

My parents and I climbed into my car. Amos came around to my side and leaned in. "We learned something else this morning," he said, frowning. "Ruby didn't set that fire. She doesn't know that Bert's box is gone."

"And I'm surprised about that," I said. With Bertha running off at the mouth, how could Ruby have missed out on that information?"

"Easy," he replied. "In a room full of customers, she can't hear hardly anything. There are too many sounds for her to sort out. That's why Bonnie takes almost all the orders. Bertha could have explained the situation in depth to her, and Ruby would have just smiled and nodded—and not picked up one single word."

"And here's another thing," I interjected. "Whoever was buried in the orchard isn't Bert Bird. So we have a body floating around somewhere. Odds are that whoever moved it set the fire. Somehow the box, the body, and Bert Bird are all connected. We have to find out how."

Amos shook his head. "I swear this thing gets goofier every day. Every time we turn over a rock, another snake crawls out."

"Amos," I said as I started the engine, "I hate to completely change the subject, but I need to bring up something else. I have a feeling—"

"Oh no," he said, standing straight and holding his hands up in surrender. "I stayed a few seconds longer than I should have."

"Let me finish. You said that there had to be someone

else connected to those cattle thieves. Someone who was planning everything?"

Amos leaned down again. "You have an idea?"

I smiled and nodded. "I have a feeling that you should check out Delbert Pennypacker. Either Bertha won the lottery, or Delbert got a job. Since neither one of those possibilities seems likely, I got to thinking. . ."

"That Delbert's been doing something *nefarious* on the side?"

I slapped him on the arm. "I knew I could improve your vocabulary with a little effort."

Amos stood up. "I'll make a little trip over to see the Pennypackers. Where are you going now?"

"We're going over to the bookstore. I want to see how things are coming along."

Amos said good-bye to my folks, gave me a quick kiss, got in his car, and drove away. I had a distinct feeling that his visit to the Pennypackers wasn't going to help my relationship with Bertha. I was trying not to worry about it as I turned the car around and drove to the bookstore. My mother interrupted my thoughts with a question about a computer.

"Mine melted in the fire, Mom," I said. "I know Elmer Buskins would let us use his."

"We brought our laptop, Ivy," my dad interjected. "Maybe we could just plug it in at your place."

"Well, let's see if we'll have any privacy first," I said. "I'm not sure if everyone's finished working."

Everything looked quiet when we pulled up in

front of the bookstore. My parents followed me up the steps and waited as I slid the key Milton had given me into the lock and opened the brand-new door. We were greeted with complete silence. No one was inside. I flipped on the light and looked around. The main room was beautiful—just as it had been before. As I looked over at the spot where Bitty's desk used to be, I got a surprise that almost made me drop my keys. Sitting a few feet away from where the old desk had been was what looked like the exact same desk! How could it be? I blinked my eyes a couple of times to make sure I wasn't seeing things. Maybe the stress of the fire and everything. . . Nope. It was still there.

"What. . .how. . . ," was all I could manage to get out.

Hearty laughter came from behind me. I turned to find Dewey standing there, enjoying my complete bewilderment.

"Something you didn't know, Ivy," he said, grinning, "was that I was with your aunt when she bought her desk. It was not long after she opened the bookstore. A farmer out near Sublette passed away, and Bitty and I went to his estate sale. We bought several pieces of furniture, including a *pair* of matching desks. I've had this one upstairs in my apartment for all these years. It's beautiful, but I have a big old oak desk I use for everything. This one was always a little too girly for me. It would make me very happy if you would take it."

I had a lump in my throat so big I couldn't get an answer out. Instead, I rushed over and threw my arms around my old friend.

"I think that means yes, Dewey," my dad said, laughing.

I nodded vigorously. "Yes. Yes, it does," I finally croaked out. "Thank you, Dewey."

He squeezed me hard before he gently pushed me away. "You're gonna get me bawlin' if I don't get out of here," he said in a husky voice. "I've got to get back to work." He walked toward the door but then stopped. "I almost forgot. I'm supposed to tell you that everything is done but that you need to stay away from the new section of flooring for a few days. Milton and his boys refinished the surrounding area so the new boards would blend in. You can put the carpet down and move the desk back when the finish dries completely."

"No problem," I said with a smile. "And, Dewey, thanks again. You don't know what this means to me."

The old man stared at me for a moment. "Yes, I think I do, Ivy. I think I do." With that, he ambled out the door, and I was left feeling blessed by God to know someone like Dewey Tater.

"Everything looks great," Dad said. "Your friends did a wonderful job."

"Yes, they did," I said. "I guess I can move back home."

My mother touched my shoulder. "Before anyone moves anywhere, let's get our laptop set up. I want to do some Googling."

I looked over at my dad and grinned. Mom had always been rather technically challenged. I wasn't sure she was up to doing a thorough search.

"Don't worry, Ivy," my dad said. "Your mother has become a Net junkie. She can surf with the best of them."

"Oh, for goodness' sake," my mother said in an irritated voice. "I am *not* an Internet junkie. I've had to learn how to use the blasted thing so we can get the supplies and things we need in China." She sighed and shook her finger at my father. "You make me sound like some kind of computer addict."

"Not an addict, dear, just a very competent researcher. If anyone can find Bert Bird in cyberspace, it's you." He looked at both of us with a serious expression. "If we locate him, what are we going to do? Have you thought about that?"

"I just want him to know how much his mother loves him," I said. "I also want to find out why he's never come home. If he really doesn't want to be here, so be it. We leave it alone and walk away. Ruby never needs to know. But if the Carvers lied to him, which I think is a possibility, it's time he heard the truth."

"I agree," my mother said, "but you're going to have to keep your word and let your father and me handle this."

"Well, I suggest we go get your laptop," I said. "I'll pack up my stuff; then we'll all come back here. I'm meeting Emily around three for coffee. I'll leave you two on your own to investigate the whereabouts of the missing Bert Bird."

"Let's go," my father said. "I feel like a part of some famous detective team." He thought for a moment. "I can't seem to think of any teams with three detectives, though."

My mother walked to the front door and pulled it open. "I can," she said. "How about Nick and Nora Charles?"

He frowned. "That's only two."

She turned and smiled at him. "You're forgetting Asta, their dog. Let's go, boy."

My dad and I laughed and followed her out to the car. As we drove back to the Biddle house, I had the strangest feeling that the search for Bert Bird would soon be coming to an end.

17

With my parents safely ensconced at the bookstore, I headed over to Ruby's to meet Emily for coffee. Although Ruby only served full meals during certain hours, she usually left her doors open so towns-folk could come inside for coffee and something already made. Bonnie served pie and cake and occasionally made a sandwich. Ruby kept the coffee going all day, though, because she felt anytime was a good time for a cup of coffee and a friendly conversation.

I pulled into a parking space right by the front door. Winter Break had been experiencing gorgeous spring weather, but we were definitely in that spring-showers-bringing-May-flowers stage. Clouds had be-gun to gather overhead, and as I stepped from my car, I felt a couple of raindrops on my arm. I had my hand on the door to the restaurant when I noticed Lucy Barber's SUV pull up across the street at Sally's Sew 'n' Such. Sally Redfield was diabetic, and Lucy almost always stopped by to see her whenever she was in town.

I knew Amos planned to talk to Lucy about the barrel tapper, but I wasn't sure how long that was going to take. I felt an urge to get answers now. I'd been pretty patient, but enough was enough.

"Lucy! Lucy, wait a minute," I hollered at her. She turned around and waved at me. I ran across the street, pelted by raindrops that were getting bigger by the second.

"Hi there," she said with a smile when I stepped under the welcome protection of the overhang in front of Sally's. "How are things going with your parents?"

"Believe it or not, they're going pretty well," I said. "My mother and I are actually talking about something besides how messed up I am."

"That's wonderful, Ivy," Lucy said. "I'm happy for you."

I couldn't help but think about how my relationship with Lucy had also improved over the last several months. She really was becoming a good friend.

"Did you need something?" she asked.

"Yes, I do," I said. "I need your help. Some weird things have been going on lately. I have a couple of questions that may seem odd. Do you mind if I ask them?"

She set her black leather bag down and frowned at me. "I. . .I suppose not," she said slowly.

"Lucy, what happened to the gas can you used to carry in your car?"

"Why, did you find it?" she asked.

"Are your initials on the bottom?"

She nodded.

"Then yes, I believe I did. When did you lose it?"

"It was Tuesday night while I was at Cyrus Pen-widdie's house. I left the back of my truck open, and when I came out, I noticed right away that it was gone."

"That was the same night as the fire at the bookstore," I said more to myself than to anyone else.

"What are you talking about?" she asked. "You're not saying that someone used *my* gas can to start that fire." Lucy's face had gone pale.

I nodded. "That's exactly what I'm saying. They used your can and then left it near the building so someone would find it."

"Why?" she asked.

"I think they were trying to make me suspect you set the fire."

"And do you, Ivy?"

"No. No, I don't." I smiled at her. "I guess whoever started the fire thought that since you and Amos used to date, I'd jump to the conclusion that you were capable of burning down the bookstore."

She nodded. "I'm glad it didn't work. You know, I was jealous of you when you first came to Winter Break. I never officially apologized to you for that, and I'm truly sorry."

I reached out and patted her shoulder. "I've had my own bouts of jealousy, Lucy. Let's just forget it, okay?"

"You've got a deal," she said and sealed it with a hug.

"I said I had two questions. Can I ask you the second one?"

She let go of my shoulders. "Sure. Go ahead."

"I noticed something in your car the other day. A barrel tapper. Can I ask you where you got it?"

"You were looking in my car? I assume it was to see if my gas can was there?"

I grinned. "Yeah, sorry."

She laughed. "I'm happy to answer your question, but next time you need to inspect my car, just ask, okay?"

I nodded. "You have my promise."

"I got the barrel tapper at a yard sale."

"A yard sale? Where?"

She hesitated, wrinkling her forehead as she thought. "Ivy, I really don't know. This past week, I've been to all kinds of sales. With the weather getting nicer, everyone and his brother is having a yard sale. If you'd looked further, you'd have seen lots of other things in my car. I buy lots of stuff in an attempt to satisfy my hobby."

"What's your hobby?" I asked.

"Tools. Old farm tools, old medical tools. Even some kitchen equipment. I think they're fascinating." She stepped out into the rain, which was falling pretty heavily by now, and opened her back car door. Then she bent over to grab something from the floorboards. She slammed the door shut and ran back to our temporary shelter. "Is this what you're talking about? Do you need it for some reason?"

I took it from her hand and looked at it closely. I was certain it was the same tapper. "Lucy, I've got to go. Someone's waiting for me at Ruby's. But would you please try to remember where you bought this? It's very, very important." I handed the tapper back to her.

"Sure, and please let me know when you find out

who set your store on fire. I'll have a few words to say to the creep."

I reached over and gave her a quick hug. "I'll do that. Thanks. Your gas can is in my car—do you want me to get it now?"

She looked up at the sky. "Looks like we're in for a real downpour. I'll get it later, if that's okay."

I thanked her again and ran across the street to the restaurant. Big raindrops chased me. I was certain I resembled a drowned rat by the time I sat down with Emily, who looked as perfect as she always did. Never a hair out of place or a wrinkle in her clothes. Emily was the kind of person I knew I could never be. I was messy and rambunctious. Emily was soft, sweet, and spiritual. And I loved her to pieces.

"I'm so glad we finally got some time together," she said while I shook the water out of my hair and all over the table.

"Sorry. I feel like a wet dog."

Her laugh was light and lilting. "Well, you certainly don't look like a wet dog. You look beautiful."

"I guess pregnant women are subject to delusions."

"Oh, Ivy, you're too self-deprecating. I've always envied your spectacular looks."

My stunned silence was interrupted by Bonnie Peavey. "Whatcha havin'?" she asked, pouring us two cups of coffee without asking. Bonnie pretty much knew what everyone wanted before they opened their mouths.

I was starving. "I hate to even ask this, Bonnie," I said, "but is there any stuffed French toast left?"

She looked over her shoulder. "There's some made up in the fridge. All I have to do is bake it. It will take about thirty minutes. Can you wait that long?"

"I'll wait as long as I have to," I said. "Are you sure Ruby won't mind?"

She shook her head. "She's not here. She had to go to Hugoton for supplies. She should be back around four thirty."

I glanced over at the dry-erase board. In big letters at the top Ruby had written: DINNER STARTS AT 6:00 P.M. FRIDAY NIGHT SPECIAL: ROAST BEEF AND RED POTATOES. Ruby served food pretty much when she felt like it. Pushing things back an hour or two was par for the course, especially when she had to do some shopping. She bought everything she could from Dewey, but he couldn't stock enough food for the kind of crowds she cooked for. Once a week at least, she would go to Hugoton for additional provisions. Usually she went in the morning. I suspected that our intense conversation after breakfast explained the late-afternoon trip.

"I'd love some French toast, too, Bonnie," Emily said. "But I think I'll have a glass of milk instead of coffee today."

"Oh, really?" Bonnie said with a smile. "Is there anything you want to tell me?"

"Not yet," Emily said with a wink.

"I'll get you that milk, honey. And maybe a little extra

French toast." With that, she took off for the kitchen.

Although it wasn't as important to talk to Emily now, since Ruby had explained the reasons behind Bert's departure, I was still curious about his relationship with Bonnie. With Ruby gone, it seemed like a perfect time to ask her a few questions. "Emily, please forgive me. I want to talk to Bonnie for a moment. I'll be right back."

Emily was used to my mercurial personality, so she just smiled and waved me on.

I swung the kitchen door open and found Bonnie pouring a glass of milk for Emily. She seemed startled by my invasion of Ruby's inner sanctum. "Did I forget something?" she asked.

"No. Listen, Bonnie, I know you told me to come by tonight to talk to you, but with the bad weather, I thought maybe you could give me a couple of minutes now. Some really strange things have been happening, and they seem to be tied to Bert Bird. Is there anything you can tell me about him?"

Bonnie stared down at her feet for several seconds before finally looking up at me and nodding. "I don't know if I can help you, but I'm willing to do what I can. Let me take this milk to Emily. I'll be right back."

I used my time alone to poke around a little in Ruby's kitchen. Everything was clean and organized. It was obvious that Ruby ran a tight ship. I could smell her tender roast beef, the aroma coming from two very large ovens. I peeked under three huge metal trays that were covered with tinfoil. Buttery boiled red potatoes sat waiting to make their appearance tonight. I'd just put the foil back when Bonnie swung the door open.

"When's Emily's baby due?" she asked.

I laughed. "You knew that because she ordered milk?"

"Sure. Emily loves her coffee. A baby is the only thing that would make her order milk."

"Well, keep it a secret. She and Buddy haven't told all their family yet."

"No problem," Bonnie said quietly. "I don't really have anyone to tell anyway."

She opened the refrigerator and took out a large tin tray of Ruby's stuffed French toast. She cut two slices, grabbed a pan, and shoved it into one of the ovens, next to a big roaster.

"Now tell me about you and Bert," I said gently after she'd closed the oven door.

Bonnie worked at tucking strands of loose, straw-colored hair under her brown hairnet. "We were only fourteen when we fell in love," she said. Each word was pronounced carefully, as if the story had been rehearsed many times. I stood close to her so the sound of rain hitting the metal roof over our heads wouldn't drown out her voice. "And yes, it really was love. To say that teenagers can't fall in love is ridiculous. My parents got married when they were fourteen. They've been together over fifty years now. Bert and I loved each other so much, it hurt. But he kept it from his mother because she was so devastated by his father's death. Bert didn't want to do or say anything to upset her. Then one day, he came to see me. I could tell he'd been crying. When I asked him what was wrong, he told me that Ruby was sending him away to stay with the Carvers. I couldn't believe it. He was so upset, Ivy. I didn't know what to do—what to say. Bert was trying to understand, but he felt abandoned. First he loses his father, and now his mother sends him away."

"But Ruby was only thinking about him, Bonnie," I said. "She was trying to protect him."

"I tried to tell him that," she said, nodding, "but he wouldn't listen. He wanted to stay here and help his mother through her troubles. He wanted to be the man of the family. Instead, she treated him like some child that needed protection." She looked at me. "Can you understand that?"

"As a matter of fact, I can," I answered slowly. "I guess I'd feel the same way."

"Sure you would. Anyway, before he left, Bert told me he loved me and that he would come home as soon as he could. He gave me a lunch box with all his most prized possessions. But I couldn't keep it. My mother didn't like Bert because she had something against Ruby. I have no idea what it was. To be honest, my mother is mad at most of the people she knows. Somehow Ruby just ended up on her list. You can imagine how happy she is that I work here." Bonnie smiled briefly. I had the feeling that upsetting her mother didn't bother her too much. "Anyway, I was certain if she found the lunch box, she'd make me get rid of it. So we decided to bury it in the peach orchard." Tears formed in Bonnie's eyes.

"Bonnie, were you with him when he buried it?"

The waitress nodded her head. "We buried it together. It wasn't easy. There hadn't been any rain for several weeks, and the ground was hard. Thankfully, we found a spot where the dirt had been recently turned over. We buried the box there."

"Did you ever think about retrieving it?"

"No."

"Because if you dug up the box. . ."

"It would mean he wasn't coming back," she said sadly.

"And the map?"

Bonnie smiled. "Did you see the picture of me in Bert's box?"

I nodded.

"It was taken at a traveling carnival that was in Hugoton. If the picture hadn't been faded, you would have seen me holding the jewelry box that Bert won for me. He put the map in there. He wanted to make sure we could find the place where we buried the lunch box."

"But how did my aunt Bitty end up with it?"

"When I moved out of my folks' place, my mother put it in the church bazaar. In fact, she donated all my things out of spite." She looked up at me. "You see, they wanted everyone in the family to stay on the homestead. But I wanted my own life, so I took a room at Sarah Johnson's. I went to retrieve the jewelry box, but I was too late. I tried to find it at the bazaar, but it was already gone. I guess it was your aunt who bought it."

"Bonnie, why do you think Bert never returned to Winter Break?"

She sighed and looked at her red, dry hands. "I don't know. I've asked myself that so many times, I can't think about it anymore. As crazy as it sounds, Ivy, I still believe he'll come back to me someday."

"Have you and Ruby ever talked about Bert?"

She shook her head. "No. She knew we liked each other, but when she told Bert she wanted him to concentrate on saving the farm instead of fooling around with me, he decided to keep our relationship a secret. His mother had been so hurt already by the loss of his dad, he couldn't stand to add anything else to her worries."

I was pretty sure Bonnie didn't know about Bert's letter asking to stay with the Carvers. She really had no idea why he hadn't kept his promise to return to her.

I stood up and pushed the stool back to where I'd found it. "Thank you, Bonnie. This information helps me. But I have one other question."

Bonnie stood up also. "Let me guess," she said with a wry smile. "Why am I still in Winter Break and why have I worked for Ruby all these years?"

"You're trying to take care of Bert's mother—for his sake?"

Once again, Bonnie pushed her straying strands of hair back into her hairnet. "It's all I have left of him," she said softly. Then she turned around and began stirring something on the stove.

I took that as my signal to leave and went back to the table, where Emily sat staring at my cup of coffee. "This milk thing is going to be a real challenge for me," she said.

I sat down and picked up my cup. The coffee was lukewarm, but I didn't care. Bonnie's story had really touched me. That kind of love. . .love that had bloomed when they were children; it was a lot like my relationship with Amos.

Emily and I spent awhile talking about our families. She told me about their search for baby names, and I told her about the plans I had for the store. Then she mentioned Faith and her concern for the young girl.

"Why don't you send her to help me in the store after things get up and running?" I said. "I could use some assistance, and it sounds like Faith needs something to do."

"I don't know, Ivy. She's quite a handful. Are you sure you want to tackle someone like her?"

"Aunt Bitty would have said yes, Emily. And so will I. There's nothing too difficult for God. If He can use me to help her, I'd consider it a privilege."

The rain spattering on the roof and the heavenly smells coming from the kitchen blended together to create a cozy atmosphere. Even though Emily and I had been apart for several years before I came back to Winter Break, it seemed as if I'd left only yesterday. For the first time in days, I felt really relaxed. Finally, Bonnie brought out two plates of Ruby's stuffed French toast. My determination to eat healthily grew little wings and flew away. I consoled myself in the belief that nothing was really off limits as long as most of the time I made good choices. An occasional treat was good for the soul. And my soul was singing, "Hallelujah!"

Emily and I ate as if we hadn't seen food in a week. Of course, Emily was eating for two. I didn't have that excuse. About halfway through I remembered why it was best to eat Ruby's food with caution. The French toast wasn't the only thing that was stuffed.

"Oh, Ivy, I almost forgot," Emily said while I was letting my fork cool down, "you wanted me to ask my mother about people who left town around the same time she did."

I really didn't need the information now, but I wasn't certain I could tell Emily that without revealing why it was no longer necessary. I'd promised Ruby that I wouldn't tell anyone about Bert, so I just nodded.

"I'm glad you asked about it, because it forced my mother to admit that she took off for a while after she graduated from high school. She wasn't sure she wanted to live in Winter Break, surrounded by Baumgartners." Emily laughed. "Somehow it made her seem a little more human to me."

"Wow. So your mom was one of the renegade Baumgartners, huh? I've heard about them, but I think she's the first one I've known."

Emily snorted. "Yeah, my mom the rebel."

I had to giggle at the idea of Inez Baumgartner as a rebel. She was about as down-to-earth and mild mannered as anyone I'd ever known.

Emily took another bite of French toast and rolled her eyes. "I've got to quit eating this," she mumbled. After a few more chews and a swallow, she took a drink of milk. "Mom said that she and her second cousin Darrel took off for Wichita. After a couple of weeks, Mom came back. She didn't like life outside of Winter Break. But Darrel stayed. He's an attorney in Topeka now."

"Wow. Someone who made it out."

She shrugged. "Yeah. At least he stays in touch. My mom's aunt Edith left Winter Break right around the same time and no one ever heard from her again."

"Edith. Are you talking about Edith Bruenwalder?"

Emily nodded. "Yes. Harvey's wife." Although the restaurant was almost empty, Emily leaned closer to me. "According to my mother, poor Edith was a very nice woman. She loved kids even though she and Harvey never had any. It was her idea to host the Scout jamborees in the orchard. Eventually Harvey shut them down out of spite. Mom suspected that Harvey abused her. She noticed bruises sometimes, although Edith did her best to hide them. When she left, no one was surprised. I'm sure she took off for her own protection. I guess she never contacted anyone again because she couldn't risk letting

Harvey know where she was." Emily reached down and picked up her bag. "My mom gave me a picture of Edith for my family album. I've got it here if you want to see it."

I wasn't really surprised to find out about Harvey, but it made me sad. I guess his mean streak wasn't anything new. He'd been working on it for most of his life. I was glad his wife got away.

Emily pulled out a large envelope then slid a picture out and put it on the table in front of me. It was a photograph of Harvey and Edith. They must have been in their thirties. Harvey was smiling, but it didn't seem to reach his eyes. Edith's smile was thin and her expression stoic. This wasn't a happy couple.

I started to hand the picture back to Emily when I noticed something that made my blood feel like ice water. "Emily," I said breathlessly. "Can I borrow this picture? I'll get it back to you."

"Why, Ivy," she said. "Of course you can, but what in the world? You're as white as a sheet."

I grabbed my purse and threw some money on the table. "I have to go. I can't explain now. I'll call you later."

With my heart thumping as if it wanted to jump out of my chest, I tucked the old photo under the protection of my shirt and ran out the front door of Ruby's. Lucy Barber was just coming out of Sally's. I put the picture in the front seat of my car and ran across the street. A bolt of lightning cracked somewhere off in the distance. By the time I got to Lucy, I was soaked to the skin. The rain had dropped the temperature several degrees. I felt as if I'd been shoved into a freezer. Through chattering teeth I asked her a question I was certain I already knew the answer to. Lucy thought for a moment but then confirmed my suspicions. I thanked her and ran to the car. It took me only a couple of minutes to get to the bookstore. I ran inside, startling my mom and dad, who were crouched over their laptop.

"Ivy!" my mother said. "You're absolutely water-logged. What—"

"Not—not now, M–Mom," I said. "You've got to dis–disconnect. I—I n–need to use the phone."

"But, Ivy," my father said, "we found—"

"Dad, p–p–please. I–I've got to c–call Amos right now. P–please—"

"You've got to call who?" a voice said behind me. Amos was standing on the rug by the front door, wiping his wet feet.

"Amos! I—I know what hap–happened! We–we've got to g–go."

"Go?" he said with a bewildered look on his face. "Go where? I just got here."

I ran over to him and pulled a jacket off the coatrack. I was shaking so hard I couldn't get it on. He took it from me and then held it out so I could get my arms in the sleeves.

I grabbed him and started pushing him toward the front door. "We're going. . . We're going. . ." I stopped, took a deep breath, and forced myself to calm down enough to say, "Amos, we're going to arrest a murderer."

18

"So let me see if I have this right," my dad said as we sat around the Biddles' kitchen, drinking coffee and trying to forget how much of Ruby's fried chicken we'd consumed after Sunday morning service. "Harvey Bruenwalder killed his wife, Edith, because he found out she was going to leave him."

It was a lovely spring day. Through the large windows and the French doors that opened onto the patio, I could see the sun sparkling off Lake Winter Break. The ducks and geese that lived there were splashing happily around in the water, celebrating winter's hibernation. I waved at Amos, who was out on the patio. He smiled and waved back at me. Then he returned his attention to what looked like an intense conversation.

"Right," I said, pulling my concentration back to my dad. "Several people knew he abused her, so when she vanished, everyone assumed she'd simply had enough and taken off for greener pastures."

"You'd think someone would have questioned it, though." My father stared into his coffee cup. "If either one of you disappeared, I'd like to think people would search for you."

"Most people just assumed Edith was hiding out from Harvey," I said. "Some of her family saw her leaving as merely another Baumgartner desertion. They just waited for her to come to her senses and come back to Winter Break. Unfortunately, no one ever followed up. It's really sad."

"So Harvey killed her and buried her in the peach orchard," he continued. "Then Bert Bird comes along to bury his box of treasures and finds a place where the ground is soft enough to dig up."

"Yep. He plants his box right on top of Edith, never knowing he was that close to a corpse."

"Who put the barrel tapper in the ground by the body?" my mother asked.

"Harvey," I said. "He couldn't take a chance of forgetting where she was. Of course, now we know why he got so bent out of shape when Amos and I dug up his orchard when we were kids. Fortunately for Harvey, we didn't get near that spot. After I found Bert's box, he removed the barrel tapper, hoping I wouldn't be able to find my way back."

"Then he took it to his sister's yard sale." My dad laughed and shook his head. "Even that went wrong for old Harvey. That barrel tapper made its way back to Winter Break when Dr. Barber bought it and put it in her car."

"But what really led you to the truth was the photo Emily showed you," my mother said. "When you saw that picture of Edith Bruenwalder, you noticed her pendant and realized it was one of the items in Bert's box."

I nodded. "That was the clue that pulled all the pieces of the puzzle together. After I spilled Bert's belongings on the ground in the orchard, I spotted the pendant in the dirt. I thought it had tumbled out of the box, but it hadn't. I'd uncovered it, and Edith, when I was digging. I'd always wondered why that medal was so dirty while the others were only slightly rusted. Now, of course, it makes sense."

"When you put Bert's things out on the table at Ruby's, Harvey saw the pendant. He knew right away what had happened," my dad said. "Boy, I would have loved to see his face."

I chuckled. "I thought he was looking that way because I'd trespassed on his property." I got up and poured another cup of coffee. The caffeine was beginning to make me jittery, but I hadn't slept much the night before. Too much excitement. I knew Amos was just as tired as I was. After dropping Harvey off at the sheriff's office in Hugoton, he'd gone all the way to Wichita. It was almost midnight by the time he'd returned last night.

"I'm glad Amos and the other deputies found Edith's remains behind Harvey's house. Now she can have a decent burial," my mother said. There was a hint of sadness in her voice.

My father shook his head. "Harvey must have moved her right after he discovered you'd been out in his orchard. I'll bet he almost had a heart attack when he realized how close you'd come to uncovering his secret."

I smiled. "I'm sure he did."

"I think he took Dr. Barber's gas can to divert suspicion in case someone figured out that the fire was purposely set," Mom interjected.

"He certainly tried to cover all his bases," my dad said. "But things didn't go the way he planned. The store didn't burn as quickly as he thought it would. The fire didn't even hide the fact that the whole thing was set just to hide the theft of those boxes. He couldn't allow anyone to get a good look at that pendant. If someone who'd known Edith saw it, it might have raised questions he didn't want asked."

"He probably took Dr. Barber's gas can because it was available. I doubt that he knew anything about your history with her," Mom said.

I sighed. "Thank goodness I didn't go too far down that road. If I'd really suspected Lucy, things might not have turned out the way they did."

"Well, it's a good thing Harvey tried to make it look like an electrical fire and kept everything near that one outlet," my father said. "If he'd poured gasoline everywhere, the whole store might have gone up like a dead Christmas tree—with you in it."

Dad's words made me shiver. That particular outcome was something I didn't want to think about.

"Bert's stuff is probably hidden somewhere at Harvey's," I said, changing the subject, "including the map he took, hoping I wouldn't be able to find my way back to Edith's grave. I hope we find everything. I'm sure Ruby will want all of it."

My mother smiled. "Yes, she probably will, Ivy, but I don't think it will be as important as it once was."

"I'm sure you're right," I said, glancing back toward Amos.

My father grunted. "This whole experience makes me want to go back to China. Believe it or not, things seemed a lot clearer there."

Mom laughed. "You mean like the time you tried to tell someone in Mandarin that you needed to buy a new pair of shoes and instead informed them that you were in the market for young children?"

"Oh, hush, Margie. It was an understandable mistake." Although he tried sound gruff, he couldn't hide a smile.

"Wow, Dad," I said teasingly. "Not a good thing for a minister to request from the local yokels. How did you get out of that one?"

"It took a lot of explaining, believe me," my mother said, still grinning. "Lucky for us, our obvious ignorance of the language smoothed things over."

I glanced at my watch again. It was almost three o'clock. Ruby had promised to come by after the last of her fried-chicken-engorged customers waddled out of her restaurant. Good thing Ruby's was closed Sunday evenings. It was the only time she really had to herself. She was going to need every second of it today.

Suddenly the doorbell rang, making me almost jump off my stool. I glanced at my parents, who looked as nervous as I felt. Since no one else moved, I got up and opened the front door.

"What in heaven's name is so important I had to come here as soon as I closed up?" Ruby grumbled when I swung the door open. "I'm missing my Sunday afternoon nap. I hope this is important."

"I think this is pretty important, Ruby," I said. "Please come in."

She clomped her way into the kitchen. "My, my," she said, looking around. "This place looks just the same as it did when Cecil and Marion lived here. Always was the prettiest house in Winter Break."

We walked through the living room to the kitchen, where my mother stood waiting. My father had gone out to the patio to alert Amos.

"Hello there, Margie," Ruby said. My mother opened her mouth, but nothing came out. Instead, she started to cry.

"Well, I must say that's a strange way to greet someone," Ruby said. "Just what in blue blazes is going on here?"

"Ruby," I said, "sit down. Please." I pulled one of the kitchen stools over to her.

"Now you're startin' to scare me, Ivy Towers," she said. With a little bit of a struggle and some help from me, she managed to wriggle up on top of the stool. It was a little high for someone of her stature.

"Ruby," I began, "there is something I must tell you. I. . .I. . ." I reminded myself to speak up so she could hear me. I had no intention of having to repeat what I was about to say. I could feel my insides starting to churn. Unless I did this quickly, I was going to end up blubbering like my mother. As it was, I couldn't look at her even though I could hear her hiccupping and sniffling behind me.

"Ruby," I began again, talking as quickly and loudly as I could without sounding like a gibbering idiot, "Ben Carver lied to Bert. He told him that you didn't want him. He told him that you had deserted him. That's why Bert wrote you that angry letter. He was striking back at you, trying to make you think he didn't need you either. Bert never knew you looked for him, and he never knew you wanted him back."

Ruby's face was ashen. "What? How could he have thought. . . How do you know this, Ivy Towers?" Her voice shook as she wriggled down off the stool. "How could you possibly know anything about this?"

I hadn't heard the French doors to the patio open, so I was startled when a deep voice came from behind me.

"She knows that because I told her, Mama."

Ruby stepped away from me, her eyes locking on the nice-looking man with salt-and-pepper hair who stood next to Amos.

I reached over to grab her in case she fainted, but it wasn't necessary. Her body was ramrod straight, and every fiber of her being was focused on her son, Bert Bird. My mother, who was overcome with emotion, snorted. In any other circumstance, I would have found it funny. But at that moment, it only caused the tears

I'd been holding in to start rolling down my cheeks.

"Is that really you, son?" Ruby asked, her voice trembling. "Have you really come home?"

Bert left Amos's side and went to his mother. "It's really me, Mama. Have I changed that much?"

Ruby reached up with a trembling hand and touched his face. "No. No, I see you, son. I see you."

With that, Bert wrapped his arms around his tiny mother and held her. They were both crying now, and I was close to snorting louder than my mother. I motioned for everyone to leave the room and let the two have their long-awaited reunion in peace. We all quietly exited through the French doors and stepped out onto the patio.

"So Bert really believed his mother had abandoned him all those years ago?" my father said to Amos after he'd pulled the doors shut behind us.

"Yes," Amos said with a sigh. "I guess the Carvers were pretty persuasive. With the loss of his dad, and his mother struggling so hard to take care of him, Bert was vulnerable."

"I have a question," I said as soon as I could get the words out. "I didn't ask Bert this last night because it seemed, well, too personal, but how did the Carvers treat him?"

Amos stood next to the wood railing that surrounded the deck. We'd stepped down toward the end of the patio so we couldn't see Ruby and Bert. "As surprising as this sounds, Bert told me they were good parents. They were strict but treated him kindly."

"I don't call lying to a child and taking him away from his mother kind," Mom said, wiping her eyes with my dad's handkerchief. "I call it cruel."

"Not much to be done about that," Dad said. "They're both dead. No one to blame. No one to prosecute."

"Bert wouldn't have allowed that anyway," Amos said. "He thinks they were just trying to protect him— keep him safe from a bad situation. Of course, it's clear that they had no right to make that decision for him and Ruby. That's something he'll have to come to terms with someday."

"It took you quite a bit of persuading to get him to return here, didn't it?" I asked.

Amos nodded. "Your mother located a few possibilities on the Internet, and I finally found him in Texas. After I got him on the phone, it took the good part of an hour to explain who I was and why I was sticking my nose in his business. But once he believed I knew his mother and that she really hadn't abandoned him all those years ago, he couldn't get a flight out fast enough. When I picked him up at the airport in Wichita, he was anxious to get to Winter Break and see her."

"And now what?" I wondered out loud. "Will he try to build a relationship with Ruby, or will he go back to Texas and get on with his life?"

Amos shrugged. "It's only a guess, but when we

first drove into Winter Break, he seemed pretty happy. He's divorced, no children, and he recently got laid off from his job. Maybe he'll decide to move back here. Try to make up for some of the time he and Ruby lost."

"Wouldn't that be something?" I said, grinning. "Bert and Ruby together again. You know, it was Bert's idea for Ruby to open a restaurant. Maybe he could help her—"

"Whoa," Amos said with a smile. "You're beginning to get ahead of yourself there, little lady. Let's give them time to get to know each other again." He put his arms around me. "You just solved two crimes, you know. When I started questioning Delbert Pennypecker about his newfound wealth, he folded like a cheap card table."

"You mean he really was behind those cattle thefts?"

"You nailed him. He's going to be spending some time away from Bertha." He grinned widely. "I'm not sure if he'll see that as punishment, though."

I felt sorry for Bertha. I also hoped she'd never find out that I had anything to do with bringing Delbert to justice.

"I wonder if Bonnie and Bert will end up getting reacquainted," I asked, changing the subject.

Amos chuckled. "He asked on the way up here if Bonnie still lived in Winter Break. I saw the look in his eye. He'll definitely drop by to see her."

"And how would you know what that look in his eye meant?" I asked teasingly.

He didn't answer me. Instead, he glanced over at my parents, who were beginning to experience the aftereffects of Ruby's fried chicken. I knew they would be dozing soon.

"Let's take a walk by the lake," Amos said.

I told Mom and Dad where we'd be, but they were already drifting away on clouds of fried chicken and mashed potatoes. I wasn't sure they heard me.

Amos grabbed my hand and guided me down the wooden steps that led to the the edge of Lake Winter Break. The ducks and geese came up to see if we had any food. When they were satisfied that we were useless to them, they swam away to pursue other possibilities.

Amos led me over to the same bench that was depicted in Marion's painting. It was the spot where Bitty sat, waving at me. I could almost feel her with me, as if she were sitting right next to us.

"I have something to say to you, Ivy," he said. I was surprised to see tears in his eyes.

"Amos, what is it?"

He hung his head slowly and stared down at the ground. "My background. . .my mother and father. During all this time we were wondering what happened to Bert Bird, I realized that in a way, I'd disappeared, too. When I went to live with my father, I was so disappointed in him. He was a drunk, Ivy. And he hit me."

"Oh, Amos."

"Instead of dealing with the hurt I'd felt because of my family, I hid it. Not only from you, but from me, too. I didn't want to talk about it. I didn't want to think about it. I disappeared on the inside, Ivy." Amos wiped his eyes with the back of his hand, and then he turned toward me. "But that's not the way to live. I don't want to lose any more time because of the past. Ruby and Bert have given up so much. I'm not willing to do the same." He reached into his pocket and took out a small velvet box. Then he let go of my hand and got down on one knee in front of me. "Ivy Towers," he said, his voice breaking, "I can't imagine living another day of my life without you in it. Will you marry me?"

I don't know who jumped up first, but I found myself in his arms, his lips on mine. It's hard to talk when you're kissing someone, but somehow I got out, "Yes! Yes! Yes!" before I was completely lip-locked and unable to speak.

Finally, we both sank back down onto the bench. Now Amos was laughing and I was crying. What a team.

"I had to step away from the past," he said. "I couldn't live inside other people's mistakes anymore. I'm not saying I'm perfect and that you won't have to slap me down once in a while, but I want you to know that I intend to do everything in my power to make you happy. You're a part of me. You always were, ever since the day I first set eyes on you."

"I feel the same way, Amos. We're not even married yet, but I understand what it means to be one person. I couldn't imagine living without you either."

Amos slipped the beautiful diamond engagement ring on my finger. It fit perfectly—as though it was always meant to be there.

Then, with a mischievous smile, he reached into his other pocket and took out another velvet box. He held it out to me, and I took it.

"What in the world, Amos?"

"Just open it. I'll explain everything."

I opened the box to find a key inside. "What's this?" I asked with a smile. "The key to your heart?"

Amos shook his head. "No. It's my step of faith. It's something I did because I believed with all my being that you and I were going to spend the rest of our lives together." His beautiful hazel eyes sought mine. "It's the key to your new home. God is giving you the desire of your heart."

I shook my head in confusion. "My new home? I don't understand. . . ."

"It's this house, Ivy. I bought the Biddle house. We're going to live here after we're married. You're going to live here now."

"But how. . .how could. . ."

He grabbed my hands. "I called Cecil and Marion. They said they'd never sold the house because they were waiting for the right people. The people God sent to them. When I told them why I wanted to buy it, they offered it to us at a ridiculous price. Way below what it's worth." Amos choked up. "Marion said that the house was meant for us, Ivy. Just like you and I were meant for each other."

I gazed into the eyes of the man with whom I would spend the rest of my life and realized that home was more than a town. It was even more than a house. Home was a place God created within our hearts.

And I was truly home.

Ruby Bird's Stuffed Berry French Toast

Ingredients:

1 loaf white bread
1 bag frozen mixed berries
8 ounces cream cheese
½ cup melted butter
10 eggs
⅓ cup maple syrup
1½ cups half-and-half

Instructions:

Spray a 9x13-inch baking pan with nonstick spray. Cut the bread into 1-inch cubes and line pan with half of the bread. (Use mushy white bread so it doesn't get too crunchy when baking.) Defrost the mixed berries and scatter over bread. Dot cream cheese over bread. Cover the berries and cream cheese with the other half of the bread. Combine melted butter, eggs, maple syrup, and half-and-half in a bowl. Mix well. Pour over the bread evenly. Chill, covered, overnight. Preheat oven to 350°F. Bake uncovered for 40 to 50 minutes.

Nancy Mehl's novels are all set in her home state of Kansas. "Although some people think of Kansas as nothing more than flat land and cattle, we really are quite interesting!" she says. "Creating Winter Break, Kansas, for the Ivy Towers mystery series has been a lot of fun. Through my research, I've learned even more about the 'Sunflower State.'"

Nancy is a longtime mystery buff who loves the genre and is excited to see more inspirational mysteries becoming available to readers who share her passion.

Nancy works for the City of Wichita, assisting low-income seniors and the disabled. Her volunteer group, Wichita Homebound Outreach, seeks to demonstrate the love of God to special people who need to know that someone cares.

She lives in Wichita, Kansas, with her husband of thirty-five years, Norman. Her son, Danny, is a graphic designer who has designed several of her book covers. They attend Word of Life Church. Her Web site is www.nancymehl.com.

You may correspond with this author by writing:
Nancy Mehl
Author Relations
PO Box 721
Uhrichsville, OH 44683

A Letter to Our Readers

Dear Reader:

In order to help us satisfy your quest for more great mystery stories, we would appreciate it if you would take a few minutes to respond to the following questions. We welcome your comments and read each form and letter we receive. When completed, please return to:

Fiction Editor
Heartsong Presents—MYSTERIES!
PO Box 721
Uhrichsville, Ohio 44683

Did you enjoy reading *Bye Bye Bertie* by Nancy Mehl?

Very much! I would like to see more books like this! The one thing I particularly enjoyed about this story was:

_____
_____
_____

Moderately. I would have enjoyed it more if:

_____
_____
_____

Are you a member of the HP—MYSTERIES! Book Club?
Yes No

If no, where did you purchase this book?

_____

Please rate the following elements using a scale of 1 (poor) to 10 (superior):

___ Main character/sleuth   ___ Romance elements

___ Inspirational theme   ___ Secondary characters

___ Setting   ___ Mystery plot

How would you rate the cover design on a scale of 1 (poor) to 5 (superior)? _____

What themes/settings would you like to see in future **Heartsong Presents—MYSTERIES!** selections? _____

_____

_____

_____

Please check your age range:
- ◯ Under 18   ◯ 18–24
- ◯ 25–34   ◯ 35–45
- ◯ 46–55   ◯ Over 55

Name: _____

Occupation: _____

Address: _____

E-mail address: _____